"Oh, Christopher, don't!"

"I'm not touching you, Lisa," he pointed out softly.

"Yes, you are. You haven't put your hands on me but once, but you touch me all the time with your eyes."

"Would you like it better if I did it like this?" He reached out and entangled his long fingers in her curls. Lisa gasped with the shock of longing he caused. His hands tightened around her curls and began pulling her toward him.

She could move, Lisa thought as she watched his face slowly come closer. She *should* move. But she didn't, and then it was too late. His lips covered hers, and she felt it clear through her bones. When her lips parted, it was an entirely instinctive reaction to him, and when they touched, she dissolved against him.

There was something so right about being kissed by Christopher, and Lisa went with the sensations. He felt her yielding and gathered her closer. Powerful feelings were opening up inside her—feelings that might have always been there but were just now coming back to life.

He began devouring her with long, hungry kisses, his hands wandering over her, stroking her. Lisa felt the most urgent need to get closer to him, and her hands ran up his back, across his shoulders, the sensitive tips of her fingers reveling in the touch of him.

Christopher took a deep, shuddering breath and looked at her with eyes still burning with passion. Then, inexplicably, his mouth curved into a sensuous, satisfied smile. "It's still there, isn't it? You're still in love with me . . ."

WHAT ARE *LOVESWEPT* ROMANCES?

They are stories of true romance and touching emotion. We believe those two very important ingredients are constants in our highly sensual and very believable stories in the *LOVESWEPT* line. Our goal is to give you, the reader, stories of consistently high quality that may sometimes make you laugh, sometimes make you cry, but are always fresh and creative and contain many delightful surprises within their pages.

Most romance fans read an enormous number of books. Those they truly love, they keep. Others may be traded with friends and soon forgotten. We hope that each *LOVESWEPT* romance will be a treasure—a "keeper." We will always try to publish

LOVE STORIES YOU'LL NEVER FORGET
BY AUTHORS YOU'LL ALWAYS REMEMBER

The Editors

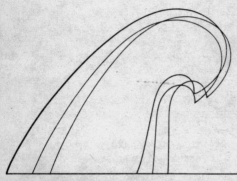

LOVESWEPT • 45

Fayrene Preston
That Old Feeling

BANTAM BOOKS • TORONTO • NEW YORK • LONDON • SYDNEY

THAT OLD FEELING
A Bantam Book / May 1984

ISBN 0-553-21644-9

Published simultaneously in the United States and Canada

Bantam Books are published by Bantam Books, Inc. Its
trademark, consisting of the words "Bantam Books" and
the portrayal of a rooster, is Registered in U.S. Patent and
Trademark Office and in other countries. Marca Registrada.
Bantam Books, Inc., 666 Fifth Avenue, New York, New
York 10103.

PRINTED IN THE UNITED STATES OF AMERICA

O   0 9 8 7 6 5 4 3 2 1

One

His presence was everywhere! He was in the unleashed fiesta of sunshine and cloudless skies that covered the Baja California peninsula on this spring day. He was in the eternal strength of the waves tumbling toward her from an ocean beyond that was a montage of surging silver-and-gray patterns in seemingly perpetual motion. And most of all, he was behind her and fifty feet up the cliff, in her uncle's cabin—the cabin that lay just south of Rosarito Beach along the old free road to Ensenada, the cabin where she and Christopher had stayed six years ago after their wedding.

"Damn!" Lisa swore aloud. But her only listener was the uncaring sea spray that misted over her every time another wave crashed into the end of the narrow jetty, just yards away. It had been four long years since she had seen him, but the very air she breathed still seemed to be filled with the entity of Christopher Saxon.

Lisa repositioned herself into the warm curve of the rock, willing her body to relax. She had really thought that she would be able to handle it. She was twenty-seven and a practicing attorney now, not some starry-eyed college student. Consequently, when Uncle William had offered her the cabin, as he had many times before, she had finally agreed, foreseeing no problems in coming back to the place where she and Christopher had honeymooned six years before.

After all, her future was looming brightly before her. She had just completed her first year with an old, established Pasadena law firm. Not only that. One of the senior partners of the firm, Robert Searcy, was in love with her and had proposed marriage. So she had accepted Uncle William's offer with the belief that it would be an excellent opportunity to put away the past once and for all before beginning the future.

But Lisa was discovering that that was not going to be quite as simple as she had first thought. Serenity didn't come easily when one had a ghost to exorcise—particularly when it was the ghost of an ex-husband.

What was it about the man that could still haunt her after four years? He was everywhere: in the bedroom of the cabin where they had first made love; in the cantina about half a mile down the dirt track toward the main road, where they had sat for hours, drinking Mexican beer and talking; on the beach, where they had taken long walks;

and even on this jetty, where they had lain in each other's arms, watching the grandeur of the Pacific, but most of all, each other.

A gust of wind blew over Lisa with a new and curious chill, causing goosebumps to rise on the skin of her arms and legs and an odd spurt of nerves to chase through her body. She sighed wearily. She'd been down here a couple of hours now; maybe it was time to go back up to the cabin. She put her tennis shoes back on and stood up, then brushed the sand off her peach-colored terry shorts and top, which called attention to her translucently pale skin and reddish-brown hair.

She was trying to ignore the strange tingling of her senses, but it wasn't working. After jumping off the jetty and onto the sand, she found herself giving in to a compulsion stronger than her own will. She just stood there, looking toward the distant blue horizon, her nails curling involuntarily into the palms of her hands. The puzzling element in the atmosphere held her captive for a moment, then she turned slowly with a strange kind of anticipation, almost a fear. A sense of the inevitable made her look up.

And there he was. On the edge of the cliff, with his legs planted wide apart and his hands stuffed into the pockets of his slim-fitting khaki pants, Christopher Saxon stood towering above her.

Lisa's vision telescoped to encompass only him, the space between them collapsing into nothingness. Their surroundings, too, disappeared; the noise receded. There was nothing left in the world but the two of them, and it might have been four minutes, not four years, since she had last seen him.

Then he moved, scaling down the bluff with a reckless speed and the surefootedness of a mountain goat. Halfway down, the steep incline sheered away to a vertical drop. Christopher took hold of the ladder that Uncle William had anchored to the side of the cliff and swung out. He completed in less than a minute the descent that had taken Lisa five careful minutes. And, as he covered the space between them with a controlled, powerful stride, the air died away, the Pacific stilled, the gulls hovered in mid-air, holding their breaths expectantly. Then Christopher stopped before her.

Four years was a long time not to see someone, Lisa reflected with an odd objectivity as she looked at him. However, at no time had there been a question of "out of sight, out of mind." No matter how hard she had fought it, he had been indelibly printed on her brain, an integral part of her dreams—dreams that privately she had termed erotic nightmares.

Now she found that four years had added muscled strength to his leanness, darkness to his golden-brown hair, steel cords to the column of his throat, charisma to his potent masculinity, and a hard cynicism to the green of his eyes. They were like marble as they collided with the blue of hers.

"You're looking well, Lisa." The velvet grit of his voice reached out and drew across her skin with the sensual effect of a silk scarf.

"What are you doing here, Christopher?"

"Lisa!" he mocked. "Is that any way to greet your long-lost husband?"

"You're not my husband."

"I distinctly remember that our wedding vows said, 'Till death do us part.' I don't know about you, honey, but I haven't died yet."

"You're the one who left me," she charged, then grimaced inwardly at herself. Where had that hurt voice come from?

There was no hurt in his voice, only a strange kind of controlled anger, as he countercharged, "You're the one who went to 'Daddy's attorney,' sweetheart. I didn't ask for the divorce. One day a stranger showed up with papers informing me that my wife of two years wanted out of our marriage." The words came out as a low, gut-ripping growl.

She went pale, and it threw the golden highlights of her tiny freckles into relief. "I repeat" —she forced the words from between clenched teeth—"what are you doing here?"

Christopher shrugged laconically. "Same thing you are, I imagine." The growl was gone, and in its place was a silky purr that vibrated along her nerve endings. "I'm on vacation."

Her glance flew to the top of the cliff, visualizing but not seeing the cabin. "But where are you staying?"

"Down the road. I've rented that little blue house at the end of the track from some neighbors of William's."

"You mean Uncle William *helped* you find a place to stay, knowing I would be here?" Uncle William was her father's brother, and she loved him dearly. Every bit as wealthy as her father, Uncle William was nonetheless totally different in personality and life-style from his brother. Her father hadn't approved of Christopher. Uncle William had.

Christopher's mouth twisted sardonically, and his eyes glittered brightly. "William had nothing to do with my renting the Monroe house. I've known that couple for quite a few years, and this isn't the first time I've stayed at their place."

Lisa's normally quick brain couldn't seem to assimilate the unexpected information fast enough. He had been down here before. But he hadn't stayed at the cabin. Maybe there were too many memories there for him . . . just as there were for her. "But you *knew* I would be here?"

He stepped within inches of her, his eyes covering her with brilliantly intense heat, and a long-forgotten weakness stabbed through her. "I didn't say that," he denied softly.

Lisa's tongue darted out to lick her lips nervously, and she was alarmed at the way his gaze followed the movement. "I don't understand."

His attention swerved to the base of her throat, where a betraying pulse hammered frantically. Then his eyes moved down to the low V neck of her shirt, darkening at the shadowy cleft revealed there. "I told you, I'm on vacation."

"Christopher!" Lisa snapped, trying to break the spell that had settled between them. "That doesn't tell me a damned thing."

His soft lips, the only part of him that seemed to have retained any gentleness, twitched with faint amusement. "What is it you want to know, Lisa?"

"I want to know," she said carefully, trying not to lose herself in his smile, "*why* you are here."

He lowered his head to within a breath of her mouth and said slowly, "I came down here to get some relief."

"R-relief?" she stammered, thinking only of the rising heat in her lower limbs.

He nodded and exhaled slightly, so that his warm breath fanned over her lips like a kiss. Lisa began to tremble. "Relief," he explained very softly. "You know, Lisa. As in an easing of an ache, or a satisfying of a discomfort."

There was hardly any space between their lips, and helplessly Lisa opened her mouth under his. But he didn't touch her in any way. Instead, he drew back a little, something in the green depths of his eyes flickering indecipherably. "I've been working extremely hard lately. I decided I needed a rest."

Lisa felt as if he had kicked her in the stomach. How could he still affect her like that? It wasn't fair, she screamed, but silently.

"Excuse me." She forced her voice to steadiness. "I've got to get back to the cabin. I hope you have a nice vacation."

He held his arms out wide, and for a second she was sure he would touch her. But he didn't. His gesture was only to indicate that her path was free.

Lisa made her way across the sand to the ladder and began to climb it, praying strength into her legs. Christopher followed right under her, and Lisa could feel the heat from his gaze on the back of her legs and through the tight material of her shorts. His face couldn't be too far from her swaying hips, she realized, he was following her so closely.

She couldn't help it. A weakness assaulted her at the erotic and totally unbidden thought; a weakness so powerful that her foot missed a rung of the ladder and she would have fallen, except for Christopher. For the first time since he had joined her on the beach, for the first time in four years, Christopher touched her. The palm of his hand braced her under her buttock, cushioning the soft roundness with the strength of his hand.

She turned to look down at him, her one leg still dangling in the air. A muscle worked along the sharply defined edge of his jaw, but he didn't speak. He just continued to support her, with the lower portion of her body resting on his hand and his fingers jutting into the division under her hip.

The heat in her veins turned her body to liquid, causing her to press heavily against his hand and making his fingers dig even deeper between her legs. Her hold tightened convulsively onto the sides of the ladder, and she moaned softly. She wasn't sure if Christopher had heard her or not, but he gave a sudden push with his hand, *forcing* her to put her leg on the rung.

Lisa finished the climb as best she could, soon arriving at the wide ledge that was the natural division of the cliff. Turning around, she waited for him to join her, which he soon did. For a long, endless moment, their eyes locked, each seeming to search for something. Then he moved ahead of her, up the cliff, easily finding the toeholds and handholds necessary to complete the ascent to the top of the bluff.

The cabin sat just a short distance away, and Lisa began to marshal her forces, intending to make it perfectly clear to Christopher that he would not be coming in. He reached the top a half minute before her and waited for her. The offer of his hand to help her the final few feet to the top was conspicuously absent.

Casting an enigmatic look toward the cabin and then back to her, he commented casually,

"Maybe I'll see you around, Lisa." With a slight nod, he sauntered off down the dirt track in the direction of the house he had rented.

Somewhat shaken by the astounding meeting with her ex-husband, Lisa took her key out of her shorts pocket and unlocked the heavy bolt of the "front door." Instead of the usual front and back door, Uncle William's cabin had a door opening out of either side of the house.

The cabin had two levels. The upper portion was actually a one-bedroom house trailer, and the lower level fit around it in an L shape. The cabin's "back door" opened into a bedroom on the lower level. Upon her arrival Lisa had made the immediate decision to use that bedroom, since she and Christopher had used the one above, in the trailer, on their honeymoon.

She walked across the long, narrow front room and threw herself down on one of the couches. Frowning at the white aluminum wall opposite her, she mulled over what had just happened.

What was she going to do? Christopher's sudden appearance put a whole new light on her staying here. Question after question formed in her mind, but unfortunately no answers followed.

Christopher had always had this power to confuse her. Normally a rational thinker, Lisa knew she had above-average intelligence and prided herself on being able to work through problems logically. Christopher was logical too, but he was a computer engineer, who thought in terms of machines, cold and emotionless. She dealt with people, who were made of flesh and blood and had real problems. Their thinking processes were entirely different, and he always seemed to defeat her.

Lisa groaned, questioning again what she was going to do. Despite the inherent memories of the place, she had been looking forward to her stay.

She could pack and leave, of course. She knew that there was an inbred reflex in people that made them want to run as far away as possible from unpleasant situations. One had only to look at the divorce statistics to realize it, and she certainly had to plead guilty to that particular charge.

In the past four years, though, Lisa had learned quite a lot, one thing being that it was a sign of character to stick with a situation, to try to seek solutions and workable compromises. Maybe the fact that she was even considering staying, showed just how much she had matured in the last few years.

It was a given fact that Christopher had been constantly in her mind since her arrival yesterday afternoon. And she knew it was impossible to run from what was in one's mind. But having him physically present and mentally present were two very different matters. If Christopher was going to be staying here, could she handle it?

Of course she could! she told herself sternly. Mulling it over, she was pretty sure that she had recovered from him. Life's most difficult lessons were the ones learned in pain, and she had learned the "Lesson of Christopher Saxon" well.

However, as long as she was soul-searching and being honest with herself, Lisa also had to admit that if there were the slightest chance that she wasn't over Christopher, now was the time to find out, before she answered Robert's proposal. Christopher had affected her today, but surely that was only because his appearance had been so unexpected. When they met again—if they met again—her guard would be up.

Having more or less made a semifirm decision, Lisa walked up the five wooden stairs into the kitchen of the trailer, casting an uninterested eye about the small room. She was hungry but didn't know what she wanted to eat and couldn't seem to gather any great enthusiasm for cooking for herself tonight. Her gaze went to the window, and she looked out at the white adobe, flat-roofed cantina sitting by the main road. The setting sun had cast a glow over the building, and it reflected terra cotta, picking up the color from the hill across the road.

Almost immediately she made another decision. The warm informality of the little café beckoned to her. Walking back downstairs, she went out her bedroom's side door to use the outhouse.

The trailer had a bathroom, but Uncle William had told her that if it was used too much, it would clog up, and somehow the thought of spending her vacation worrying about an overflowing toilet didn't appeal to her. Besides, the outhouse had a wonderful view of the ocean, unrestricted by a door and only partially screened by the branches of a tree, and it was sort of fun to rough it for a while.

Right outside her bedroom door, Uncle William had built an outdoor shower. Heated by solar panels jerry-built on the roof, the water was warm now as Lisa stood under the spray and washed the afternoon's sand out of her hair and off her smooth, supple body. Anyone walking around the back of the cabin would be able to see her, but this was the start of the week and there were very few people about.

The dirt track served as a road for the line of small houses and trailers that stretched along this particular parcel of land. Numbering about ten in all, most of them were owned by Americans who came down for holidays and weekends. Tourists came down mostly on the weekends and in the summer, and the people who lived here year round would either be working at this hour or at home.

Padding back into her bedroom, Lisa locked the door by simply dropping a board across it. The cabin was furnished with only odds and ends. There was a general rule of thumb for people with holiday cabins in Baja: Never leave anything in them that you wouldn't want to lose. Cabins up and down the coast were broken into every day, but generally only when they were unoccupied. Lisa wasn't afraid to stay by herself, but she had promised Uncle William that she would not take any unnecessary chances.

Shaking her shoulder-skimming dark auburn curls free of water, Lisa left them to dry naturally. She put on a pair of jeans and a light-orange knit top. Adding a sweater, because she knew the night would be chilly, she left the cabin.

Even though Uncle William had told her that the cantina was under different ownership from when she had last visited, it was much as she remembered it—bare floors, straight-back chairs grouped around wooden tables, and a bar that separated the kitchen from the rest of the café. Only two tables were occupied, one by a Mexican family and the other by two men, who were deep in discussion.

The bar was empty too, with the exception of a man perched on a stool. He was drinking beer and talking casually through the passthrough behind the bar to a man and woman who were cooking there. He was a man whose powerfully athletic body and ruggedly attractive face instantly attracted attention.

Christopher, of course! She hadn't heard a car go by, so she assumed he had walked over, just as she had. When the screen door slammed behind her, he turned and watched from under hooded lids as she made her way to a small table in the corner.

She gave the waiter an order for beer and tacos and then settled back to watch with a thudding heart as Christopher ambled over, beer in hand. Picking up a chair directly across the table from her and twisting it around, he threw one leg over and straddled it, his arm laying along the back of the chair.

"You cut your hair," he said, as if that were where they had left off their conversation a couple of hours before.

"Several years ago," she said, irritated at herself for barely being able to restrain herself from asking whether or not he liked her hair shorter.

He put his beer down on the table and took a pack of cigarettes from his shirt pocket. Lighting one, he inhaled deeply, all the while pondering her hair. "It's nice," he finally commented, then immediately qualified the statement, "even though I think I liked it better when it hung past your shoulder blades. A man likes something to run his hands through, you know."

Lisa smiled sweetly. "Fortunately, I'm no longer concerned about what you like and don't like. The nice judge took care of that for me."

He took a long drag on his cigarette and returned her smile. His smile was about as charming as the deadly sharks that swam the depths of the Pacific only a mile or so away, and she knew immediately that she had made a mistake in again bringing up their divorce.

"Pretty damn quick, too, didn't he? What was the matter, Lisa? Was your daddy so afraid that if he gave us a few months to think things over, we might give the marriage another chance? He used his money and his influence to expedite the matter awfully fast, don't you think?"

"Daddy didn't do anything I didn't ask him to do. He had nothing to do with our divorce, and you know it. It was those damned computers of yours!" she sputtered defensively, surprised to find that the pain she thought she had buried four years before was just under the surface of her skin. "You were always at work . . . and the rare times you did manage to come home, you wanted me in your bed, waiting passionately for you."

"As I recall, you usually were. Passionate, that is," he taunted.

She could feel herself flushing at the truth of his words, and hurried on. "You never just talked to me."

"I was usually tired, Lisa."

Surprised to notice suddenly that he sounded tired now, she nevertheless retorted, "Practically the only attention you gave me was when we made love."

"I could never get enough of you." His deep, gritty voice sent shivers of remembrance up her spine.

"If you want to know the truth," she flung at him, attempting to block the memories, "I got to where I resented the hell out of our lovemaking. It seemed like that was all you wanted me for. You weren't even interested in hearing about my studies."

"When I was home, I wanted all your attention. I loved you." His simple, flat statement took her breath away, but the past tense he had used—"loved"—hurt oddly.

Charges and countercharges. After four years, what good would they do? Yet still they came. "So much that you couldn't stand the thought that I might actually want a career of my own."

"You were the daughter of a rich man, Lisa. You'd never had to earn a penny in your life. I just didn't think you were really serious about it."

"Oh, right," she snapped sarcastically. "No one could be serious about a career but you. I think you used your poverty as an excuse for the obsession you had with those computers you used to play with so much."

"I wasn't *playing*. I was trying to make something of myself, Lisa," he flared briefly, "to prove to your father, and to you, that I could earn a decent living and support you as well as or better than he had all your life."

"All I ever wanted was you. . . ." Lisa's voice trailed off as she realized what she had just said.

An uncomfortable silence lay heavily between them. Recriminations and bitterness were like cancer. Once started it was hard to stop it from spreading, inflicting more and more damage to the body, until it was completely destroyed.

Finally Christopher spoke. "You were young, Lisa. So was I." His voice carried across the table, soft and compassionate and faintly unnerving. He looked down at the table for a moment, tapping his cigarette into an ashtray and giving Lisa a chance to *think* instead of *react*.

She could disagree with nothing that he had said. She had been twenty and just about to begin her third year in college when Uncle William had introduced her to his new employee. At twenty-six years of age, Christopher had been very impressive to the young girl she had been then. Hell! She wasn't a young girl any longer and he was *still* impressive.

Granted, she was no courtroom attorney, but she didn't usually let people put her on the defensive like that. Only Christopher had ever been able to do it, and the reason was simple. She had once been very much in love with him.

Christopher took another deep draw on the cigarette and exhaled slowly, looking at her through the haze of the smoke. "Lisa . . . I think it's pretty obvious that we blame each other for what happened between us. And there's no question but that we've both suffered. But rehashing it, reopening old wounds, isn't going to solve anything. Do you agree?"

She nodded cautiously.

"For whatever reason," he continued quietly, "we both happen to be in a place where we were once quite happy. Let's not spoil those memories."

Lisa looked at her ex-husband with astonishment. That hadn't sounded like the Christopher Saxon she had once known. He had spoken haltingly, as if he were giving a great deal of thought to what he was saying.

At any rate, she agreed with him. Nothing they could do or say would change what had happened four years ago. They had once loved each other deeply and there had been a lot of things right about their marriage. How could they continue to tear each other apart and still be able to retain any of the good and positive things that they had shared? If they lost all of that, then it would mean there had been no value to their love. And despite everything, Lisa would never accept that.

The food came, and while she ate, they talked of this and that, consciously avoiding anything that might set them off again. There was something unnatural about the two of them speaking so stiltedly of trivialities, Lisa reflected, just as if they were strangers and hadn't at one time shared incredible intimacies.

When she finished, he asked, "Can I walk you home?"

The old Christopher never would have asked. She nodded, unable to voice any of her somewhat nebulous thoughts at the moment.

Once they cleared the cantina's yard, the night closed in around them, clear and cool, as they strolled toward the cabin. There were no streetlights to mark their way, only the light from the moon and the stars, and Lisa was glad the darkness shielded her confusion. "How long have you been down here?" she questioned curiously.

"I just got here last night. The traffic coming across the border into Tijuana wasn't too bad on a Monday. Everyone was going the other way."

"I know. I found pretty much the same situation this morning when I came through," she commented before she realized he hadn't asked her when she had gotten here. Perhaps he just didn't care. "They say that the Tijuana border is the busiest in the world. It looks like it's a fascinating place, but I'm not sure I'd ever want to stop there. For one thing, the chaotic traffic patterns, plus those little kids darting in and out between cars trying to sell things, make me nervous, and for another, I saw two fights break out within a block of each other while I was driving through."

"It's colorful, all right, but I think it's safe enough if you keep to the tourist hangouts."

It was like discussing the weather, she thought. Once you exhausted the topic, the conversation died an abrupt death. Lisa searched her mind for something else to talk about. "So what all have you got planned for your vacation?"

There was a minute of silence when the only noise was the crunch of their feet against the gravel and the distant roll of the ocean.

When he answered, it was casually enough, but his tone had become guarded. "Oh, I don't know. I really haven't planned that much. How about you?"

"Pretty much the same. I thought if I got terribly energetic, I might drive down to Ensenada for a day."

"Really?" His voice took on new animation. "That sounds like fun. Maybe we could go together."

His suggestion caught her off guard. "Yeah . . . well, maybe."

They reached the cabin door, and Lisa unlocked it. She had left one light and Uncle William's old radio on downstairs. It received only one station, an FM station that broadcast mood music out of San Diego. Lisa couldn't remember if she had even turned it off since she had arrived. Somehow the soft tinkle of a piano and the velvet strings of a violin harmonized perfectly with the roar of the ocean and the cry of the sea gulls.

Turning, she found Christopher watching her. "What's the matter, Lisa? Don't you think that two people who have been lovers can be friends as well?"

"What are you talking about?"

"I'm talking about spending some of our vacation together."

"But that's ridiculous!" She leaned back weakly against the doorjamb. He followed, resting one hand beside her head and bringing his face close to hers.

"Is it?" His voice sounded hushed in the intimacy of the night.

"We're divorced, Christopher."

"Okay, lady, you're the lawyer, you tell me—is there some law that says that two consenting adults who just happen to have been married at one time but who are now single can't spend some time together if they want to?"

She eyed him suspiciously. "What are you trying to do?".

He lowered his body until it was almost, but not quite, touching hers, supporting his weight with his forearm above her head. "Not a damn thing, honey, that you don't agree to."

Her pulses began to stir urgently, and a warmth sprang up under her clothes at the closeness of his body to hers. "It's been four years, Christopher. I've changed and I'm sure you've changed. We don't even know each other any more."

"But don't you think it would be fun to get reacquainted?"

She ran her tongue over her dry lips. "Fun is probably not the correct word to use in our case."

"Interesting?" he offered.

"I—I'm not sure. There may be too much hurt in the way."

He shifted his weight slightly, making her body tremble with anticipation, but still he didn't touch her. "We could give it a try, Lisa. What have we got to lose?"

What could she say? My heart, my body, my soul! No, she couldn't say that—even if it was the truth. She tried flippancy. "I guess dating one's ex-husband could be a novel approach to a vacation."

He ignored it. "I know there's pain, however

deep or shallow its grave. Don't forget, I was there too. But we'll take it slow."

She nodded, unable to speak.

"Do you want me to light you a fire before I go?" His breath whispered over her face like a touch in itself.

"No."

"Do you want me to go?"

"Yes."

He straightened, never having actually touched her. It had only felt as if he had.

"Good night, Lisa."

Two

Even though she didn't entirely understand the hodgepodge of emotions that were entangling her mind, Lisa slept well and awoke late to a day swathed with a golden promise and a healthy irreverence for the fast-paced life she lived back in Pasadena. Dressing in another pair of jeans, but this time topped by a camel boat-necked blouse, she ambled up to the kitchen to make coffee, careful to use bottled water for everything she ate or drank.

A knock took her back down the stairs to find Christopher at the side door, a paper bag in hand. "You're up early," she observed mildly, not completely certain how to act toward him.

"Have you looked at the time, sleepyhead? It's ten o'clock, and I've already been into town to the Panaderia. Wait until you see what I got for our breakfast." While he was talking, he had let himself in, whisked upstairs, and returned with paper plates, the coffeepot, and two mugs, setting them down on the table in front of the window. "I think I bought two of everything; I just couldn't resist the delicious smells."

Lisa moved from the door to the table, where he was removing pastries from the bag and putting them on a plate. "Breakfast? Together?"

"Had you planned something else?" He straightened and eyed her intently.

Chewing on her bottom lip, she answered hesitantly, "Not really."

"Good." He nodded briskly, apparently not willing to delve too deeply into her obvious ambivalence this morning.

He held a chair out for her, seated her, and then sat down himself. The middle pane of each of the mullioned windows that marched along the front wall of the cabin opened out. There wasn't even a screen to hinder a single beam of sun or puff of salt-scented air from entering the morning-warmed room.

Lisa attacked the still-hot pastry with sudden enthusiasm. "This is delicious. Did you get it at that little bakery where we used to go?" The words were out before she realized what she'd said. In no way did she want to bring up the time when they had been here last.

"Yes, and I found a tortilla factory on a side street where we can go later if you like. You can see them making them through a window in the side of the building."

Not by so much as a flicker of an eyelash had Christopher indicated that he had been affected by the reminder of their honeymoon. Yet Lisa realized that he too must have the feeling that by agreeing to spend some time together they were walking, however carefully, through a mine field. It only stood to reason that they would hit a mine now and again. Whether or not they could withstand the explosion, or even whether it mattered, remained to be seen.

She took another bite of her roll. "What have you been up to, Christopher?"

The dark green of his eyes flashed briefly with amusement. He must have guessed that Uncle William couldn't help but mention him from time to time, even though Lisa had always had the definite suspicion that her notoriously absent-minded uncle carefully screened the information he passed on. "I split off from William's company a few years back—with his complete blessing, I might add."

Lisa had heard that.

"Your uncle has been a good friend to me as well as an excellent teacher."

"He has always said you were brilliant," Lisa commented generously.

"I don't know about that"—he shrugged with unassumed modesty—"but I've had some ideas that have paid off."

"Oh? Like what?"

He shot her a sharply mocking look. "You were never interested before."

They had hit a mine. The tiny white rays in the blue of her eyes turned steel gray with quick anger. "Maybe I wasn't . . . or maybe it was just that I was afraid to ask because I knew you didn't credit me with enough intelligence to understand your explanations."

"Oh, yeah? Well, maybe *I* didn't want to waste what little time we had together, thanks to your schooling, discussing business."

Lisa opened her mouth to retaliate, but Christopher unexpectedly held up his hand with a resigned gesture. "I'm sorry, Lisa." His mouth lifted in an attractive, self-deprecating grin. "No one said this was going to be easy, right?"

She nodded and looked down at her coffee cup, trying to control her heartbeat, which had increased in speed at his smile. No. Whatever it was that they were trying to do, for whatever reason, it was *definitely* not going to be easy.

He continued matter-of-factly. "I've developed an integrated-circuit memory chip that is guaranteed to create a sensation in the computer industry. It will hold twice as much data in the same space and operate at the same speed as those in use now. I've already had several offers."

"That's marvelous, Christopher," she said sincerely. "I'm really happy for you. Not everyone gets to see a dream come to fruition."

He finished eating and lit a cigarette before he

said, "You have, I understand. William tells me
that you have an excellent position with a respected
law firm in Pasadena."

"Yes, I was lucky. They've been great to work
with. I've learned a lot."

"William also tells me that there's a serious relationship between you and one of the senior partners . . . an older man, I believe."

Evidently Uncle William had not bothered to
screen the information he passed on about her,
Lisa thought with irritation. And why had Christopher stressed the word "older"? "Robert's not
that old!" she retorted defensively. "Well . . . maybe
a little more than ten years older than you are.
But he's a wonderful man, completely settled and
enormously stable." She didn't add, "and sometimes very dull."

"Is that what you want, Lisa?" Christopher asked
quietly.

"I think he's good for me," she said, then added
before stopping to think, "And what about you?
Are you interested in anyone at the moment?"

Her heart sank heavily at his affirmative nod.
"I've been seeing a very lovely lady for quite some
time now."

Lisa didn't know what she had expected, but
certainly not the stabbing pain that shot through
her at the thought of Christopher's loving someone else. It was almost incomprehensible that,
given what they had once had, he could care for
another woman. She gave him what she hoped

looked like a bright smile. "Are you going to marry her?"

His green eyes gazed at her steadily. "I've thought about it."

Lisa licked her lips. "I see. More coffee?"

"No, thanks."

Lisa turned to stare unseeingly out the window. She had experienced a lot of different emotions since first seeing Christopher on the beach the day before. And now sadness had been added to all the others. Unselfconsciously she quietly began to speak her thoughts.

"Time seems to have this way of passing without our even being aware of it. When you're young, you feel as if the world was made fresh and full of hope just for you. Only, at the time, most of us are too immature to realize just how fleeting everything really is. We don't understand that if we don't hold on tightly to those things that we value most highly, one day we're going to turn around and they'll be gone."

"What are you trying to say, Lisa?" Christopher's voice was oddly gentle.

She looked back at him. "I don't know."

Their eyes met across the old formica table, searching for answers when there weren't even any questions as yet.

Christopher broke the silence. "Shall we go into town this afternoon and shop a bit, maybe stop for a drink at the hotel?"

"Okay." She surprised herself by agreeing. "Just

let me do a little sweeping out first. There must be an inch of sand and dust in this place. I don't think Uncle William's been down in a while."

"I'll help. The owners of the house where I'm staying were down last week and left it pretty clean."

Cleaning the cabin was simply a matter of sweeping the brown concrete floors and shaking out the various scatter rugs and the colorful cotton throws that covered all the couches and chairs. Lisa and Christopher worked unpredictably well together, and were soon finished and on their way to the small resort town of Rosarito Beach.

Christopher helped her into his late-model Mercedes, responding with a rueful twist of his mouth to her raised eyebrows.

"Don't worry!" she reassured him soothingly. "I wouldn't *think* of reminding you that you used to say you'd never own one of those 'damned status-symbol cars.' "

"I didn't get this car because it's a status symbol," he grumbled good-naturedly. "I got it because it's a good investment and a helluva car."

"Well, *of course* you did! Did I say you didn't?" she asked innocently. "By the way, don't look now, but your big, shiny 'investment' is covered with a thick coating of reddish-brown dust."

"You've got no room to talk. Have you noticed that you can't even *see* your car now?"

"Yes, but I don't have to worry because my car doesn't mind the dirt. It's just a little ol' Mustang.

You, on the other hand, had better be careful. Your car may get fighting mad over the indignities it's being made to suffer south of the border."

"Just so long as you don't get mad at me," he returned, so softly that Lisa wasn't sure she had heard him right.

They made their way out of the ranchero, past the cantina, and turned north on the old free road—Highway 1. The narrow, two-lane road passed nothing but the ocean at first, and then Popotla, a seaside settlement that was home to a large trailer park, came up on the left. Popotla was soon followed by an array of colorful curio shops, which decorated the road right on into town.

"Would you like to stop at any of these little shops?" Christopher asked.

"Yes, I think I would. I saw them as I was coming in yesterday, and they looked irresistible."

"Don't get in too much of a hurry to spend all your money," he teased. "I'm pretty sure these smaller shops don't take credit cards."

"I know this is going to be a shock to you, Christopher, but I don't have any credit cards anymore."

"Just my luck!" he moaned, pulling up in front of a line of curio shops. "You waited until *after* we were divorced to throw away your credit cards. I think I just paid off the last of your bills the other day."

"Liar," she kidded back as she hopped out of the car and ran into the nearest shop.

The afternoon passed quickly while they bargain-hunted among the varied goods that were offered. Since it wasn't their peak season, the shop owners were anxious to make deals, and Lisa enjoyed trying to get lower prices on some of the items.

It was strange how, after being apart four years, they were attracted to the same things. Lisa would see a piece of pottery, a basket, or a stone carving that she thought might go well in her apartment and head for it, only to find Christopher meeting her there. More than once they broke into gales of laughter when they ended up at the same item.

The only time Lisa felt a little funny about being with Christopher was when she noticed him looking at a particularly beautiful dress. Light periwinkle blue, square-necked, and flowing to the floor, it was made out of a soft cotton. Blue flowers were embroidered around the hem and the cuffs of the sleeves. She quickly turned away, jealousy raging in her at the thought of his buying the dress for the woman he was thinking of marrying.

Somewhat later, engrossed at a counter as she contemplated a leather billfold for Robert, Lisa was surprised to feel a tap on her shoulder. She turned, expecting to see Christopher, but instead, all she could see was a huge bouquet of dozens of paper flowers *standing* in front of her. Each flower measured over a foot and a half across and each was a different color.

A disembodied voice that sounded suspiciously like Christopher's gasped, "Since we've single-handedly managed to raise the standard of living in this little town in the last couple of hours, what do you say we adjourn to the hotel for a drink?"

She grinned and addressed her remark to the bouquet. "But what will we do with the flowers?"

"We can leave them in the car."

"Will they all fit?"

"That's one of the beautiful things about *investment* cars," the voice answered cheerfully. "They have lots of room for flowers!"

Laughing, they stuffed their packages in the trunk and filled the back seat with the flowers. Then, getting in the car, they drove the short distance down the Avenida Juarez to the over-fifty-year-old Rosarito Beach Hotel.

Walking through the white arched doorway that had "Bienvenidos" printed over it was like taking a trip back in time, Lisa thought delightedly. She fully expected to see Heddy Lamarr and Charles Boyer, wearing tropical white and sitting in fan-backed rattan chairs under a slowly moving ceiling fan, plotting intrigues together.

The interior of the hotel was dark and cool and decorated with richly-colored tiles. A full-sized mural covered one wall of the reception area. They made their way through the charming old-time glamour to the Aztec Room. Great arches filled with plate glass let diffused lighting into the dining room. At the same time, they allowed a view of the long, narrow rectangular swimming pool and the clear plexiglass sea wall beyond that protected swimmers and sunbathers from the blowing wind and sand off the Pacific.

"Are you hungry?" Christopher asked.

"No. Unless you are, why don't we go out to the Beachcomber Bar?"

The bar curved out onto the beach and was enclosed by glass. A small combo played in a deep corner, as Christopher and Lisa sank into thickly padded chairs with wide rattan armrests.

"What will you have?" Christopher asked, scanning the bar list.

"Something properly exotic, please, with flowers, fruit, and paper umbrellas hanging all over it."

"I think you've got enough flowers, don't you?"

"Well, then"—she waved her hand through the air—"just fruit and paper umbrellas . . . but lots of them."

"She'll have a glass of paper umbrellas," he told the attentive waiter, "and I'll have two Piña Coladas." He looked back at Lisa. "Would you like a snack? We missed lunch."

"What flavors do your umbrellas come in?" she asked the young Mexican waiter, who was no doubt used to the peculiarities of *Norteamericanos.*

Christopher broke in. "We'll just have a large plate of shrimp. *Gracias.*"

Lisa looked down her nose at him. "I do believe

you've gotten respectable since you've become a success, Christopher."

He grinned at her. "And I do believe that when you're not angry, you can still be more fun than anyone else I know."

Her senses quickened, and she just had to ask, "Does that include the future Mrs. Saxon Number Two?"

"Fishing, Lisa?"

"Me?" she asked with what she hoped was an appropriate amount of virtuous surprise.

Much later that afternoon, while driving back to the cabin, they passed Calafia, an attractive mobile-home community. "Would you like to come back here this evening for dinner?" Christopher asked. "I understand it's very good." He was referring to not only the conventionally enclosed restaurant there, but a series of individual dining terraces that spilled down the cliff to the ocean.

Suddenly a little uncomfortable with his assumption that they would dine together, she answered, "I think I'll just eat at the cabin tonight. Uncle William was telling me about a little fishing village just to the south called Puerto Nuevo. He said if I got there in the afternoon when the fishermen were coming in, I could buy whatever they'd caught on that particular day. I thought I'd see if I could get some halibut to cook this evening."

"That sounds delicious. I've got some wine I

could contribute. Did you bring anything to make a salad with?"

"Y-yes."

"Cornmeal for cooking the fish?"

"Uncle William keeps some at the cabin in an airtight container." Even to Lisa's ears, her voice had a decidedly cold edge to it.

"Great! We've got the makings of a first-class dinner."

"I don't remember inviting you," she snapped.

Christopher took his eyes off the road and looked at her for a moment. "Didn't you?"

Something in his green eyes made her stomach clench with the jarring knowledge that, even if she hadn't invited him, she wanted to be with him tonight. "Yes," she answered softly.

Lisa sat alone on the couch, peering from beneath her lashes at Christopher. Sitting directly across from her in Uncle William's easy chair, he appeared completely relaxed, sipping a glass of wine and staring pensively into the fire he had lit before dinner.

The disturbingly intimate atmosphere was enhanced by the fact that the only other light in the cabin glowed dimly from a kerosene lamp that hung from the ceiling halfway down the length of the front room, plus several candles. A soft melody called "I Will Remember You," floated down the room to them from the radio. That was the trouble, Lisa reflected ruefully. She *did* remember. Only too well. But she didn't want to remember.

To get her mind off how happy she and Christopher had been the last time they had stayed in the cabin, she remarked conversationally, "The colors in the flames are beautiful."

Christopher switched his attention to her so quickly, it led her to believe that his mind had never been far from her. "It's the driftwood I added. When the water evaporates from the wood, it leaves salt deposits and other minerals, causing the fire to burn blues and greens."

She heard his explanation with part of her mind, but with the other part she acknowledged that the green flames in the fireplace exactly matched the ones in Christopher's eyes as he looked at her. The brilliance she saw there sent a surge of excitement rocking through her. She tore her gaze away, forcing it back to the fireplace. "It's really beautiful, isn't it?"

The fireplace stretched across the end of the cabin. On either side of it, the stonework wall rose to the ceiling, encrusted with rocks that had been found on the beach. The hearth was wide and high, and a deep copper hood came down over the opening, with abalone shells studded across the top of it.

"Yes, it is. This whole place is interesting."

His deep voice sounded too close, and she turned to see that, without her being aware of it, he had moved onto the couch beside her. His nearness was an aphrodisiac to her already alert senses. The raw maleness of him spanned the short space that now separated them, making her conscious of the slightest details about him, right down to the even pattern of his breathing.

In her nervousness, she began talking, saying the first thing that came into her mind. "Thank you for the dress." Before they had parted to wash and change for dinner, he had tossed her the package with a nonchalant, "This is for you."

Now he gave a little nod. "It looks beautiful on you, but then, I knew it would. Your skin has a delicate quality that I always thought was complemented by bright colors."

She took a deep breath through lungs that didn't seem to be working properly. "I—I spent a couple of weeks down here one summer when I was younger, and Uncle William told me the history of the place."

"Really?" Christopher questioned with a lazily amused smile, obviously aware of her discomfort.

"Y-yes. Years ago, it seems, the governor of Baja granted a 'Donship' and this land to the father of the present owner. But the government put a few restrictions on it. They didn't want any foreigners ever owning the land or building permanent structures on it. But they determined that trailers would be okay, because trailers could be moved easily, and, at the same time, they also decided that they didn't mind if people wanted to build structures onto or around the trailers. Since they looked on trailers as impermanent, they felt that the whole thing could still be moved.

"Uncle William leases the land from Don Pancho's son, but he owns the structure. One summer he and a couple of fishermen built the fireplace."

Christopher's eyes had dropped to the revealing neckline of her dress. "William has told me that story before. Where did the mariachis come from?" he questioned, referring to three fat little plaster men sitting on top of the mantle but not looking at them.

"There's really no telling," Lisa managed faintly, directing her gaze anywhere but at him. "You know Uncle William as well as I do. All sorts of people stay here."

"Including us when we were on our honeymoon."

It was the tone rather than the words that made her finally look at him. His gaze was roaming over her with hot intent, and an exquisite weakness oozed into her already overheated blood.

"It's been four years, Christopher," she whispered weakly.

"Sometimes it seems like only minutes." The normal grittiness of his voice had softened to a flowing silk, and his eyes were holding hers in a grip of desire.

"Don't!"

"I'm not touching you, Lisa," he pointed out softly.

"Yes, you are. You haven't put your hands on

me but once, but you touch me all the time with your eyes."

"Would you like it better if I did it like this?" He reached out and entangled his long fingers in her curls. "Or like this?" He placed his palm over her breast, catching her completely off guard, and Lisa gasped, such was the shock of longing it caused. His hand tightened around her curls and began pulling her unhurriedly to him.

She could move, Lisa thought vaguely as she watched his face slowly come closer. She *should* move. But she didn't, and then it was too late. His lips covered hers, and she felt it clear through to her bones. When her lips parted, it was an entirely instinctive reaction to him, and when their tongues touched, she dissolved against him.

There was something hellishly right about being kissed by Christopher, and Lisa went with the sensations. He felt her yielding and gathered her closer. Powerful feelings were opening up inside her—feelings that might always have been there yet were just now coming back to life, like tiny flowers reopening to the warming caress of the sun.

His hand stroked her breast through the blue cotton and she twisted her body in response, unintentionally pushing more fully into his hand. Christopher had been right. It was as if they had been parted only minutes instead of years. It was shocking how her body seemed to remember his;

shocking because she had done her level best to forget.

He was devouring her with long, hungry kisses. His hands were wandering over her, touching, cupping, squeezing, molding, and, most of all, thrilling her beyond thought. She had the most urgent need to get even closer to him, and her hands ran up under his knit shirt, stroking across his back, the sensitive tips of her fingers reveling in the smoothness of his skin.

Her heart was pounding violently, and she just managed to stop herself from crying out when he abruptly pulled away.

He took a deep, shuddering breath and looked at her with eyes still burning with passion. Then, inexplicably, his mouth curved slowly into a sensuous smile of satisfaction. "It's still there, isn't it?"

She didn't answer him. How could she? She was too stunned. Never, not once in the last four years, had she considered the possibility that Christopher's kisses might still have the power to shake her beyond belief. But they did, and she now knew how very wrong she had been not to consider it.

Bringing her against him one more time, he kissed her tenderly. "Good night, Lisa."

Three

The night had brought no sleep and the morning brought no peace. Lisa roamed restlessly over the cliffs above the Pacific with one thought in mind: *what now?* It was the same question that had kept her tossing and turning all night. The same question that seemed to have no resolution.

Her mind was spinning and her senses were whirling. Had last night really happened? After all these years? The fact that Christopher had kissed her had been mind-boggling enough, but her reaction to his kisses was really staggering. And, as if that weren't sufficiently disturbing, she had to deal with the lingering knowledge that somehow, in some way, none of it had been enough.

It couldn't be happening again! Not those old feelings that threatened to swamp all her senses, those feelings that a much younger Lisa had had and that the older Lisa had been so sure she had gotten over. Well, she wouldn't let it happen again, she told herself sternly. She was older and wiser. And besides, surely too much pain had passed between them to let them go back, and most certainly too much had changed for each to let them go forward.

Lisa became aware of voices. Looking up, she saw a man lounging behind the cantina. She couldn't see whom he was talking to, but she veered toward him, consciously seeking a diversion in the form of another human being—someone other than Christopher, that is.

"Good morning," she called.

"*Buenos días, señorita*," the man returned slowly.

"Uh . . . it's *señora*." Oh, damn! Why had she felt the need to say that? Even though she had been married, she wasn't now. She could claim to be a *señorita*, couldn't she? Oh, hell, what did it matter anyway?

The heavyset man seemed to agree with her mental conclusions, because he simply shrugged. He was sitting with his chair propped up against the adobe wall, enjoying the sunshine, a straw hat tilted over his eyes.

Just then a small boy more or less fell out the door, struggling with a trash can that was almost bigger than he was. Lisa rushed over to him, taking one of the handles and helping him set it down.

He smiled shyly. "*Gracias, señora*."

Liquid dark eyes stared out at her from a face

that seemed much too thin. Lisa held out her hand to him. "Can you speak English?"

"*Sí, señora.*" Hesitantly, he took her hand. "*Mi madre* taught me."

"What's your name?"

"Patricio."

"Well, Patricio, I'm glad to meet you. My name is Lisa. That seems like an awfully big trash can for you to be carrying. How old are you?"

He squared his painfully frail shoulders. "I will be eight very soon."

"Patricio," the man bellowed at the same time that his beefy arm reached out and he forcefully smacked the child on the back of the head. "Get back to work."

The boy cast a weary look toward Lisa with eyes that were smarting with tears, then turned and went back into the cantina.

"No good, lazy *muchacho*," the man grumbled. "Don't know why I put up with him."

Lisa was indignant. "You didn't have to hit him!"

"Do not trouble yourself, *señora.* He's used to it. He'd never do any work if I didn't beat him now and then."

"Is he your son?"

He waved a dismissive hand. "He was my sister Blanca's *niño.* She died a few months back"—he piously crossed himself—"and I had to take him in."

"You *had* to?"

"No one else wanted him."

Lisa felt a surge of frustration. "Surely in this day and age, when there are couples who so desperately want to adopt children, you could find a good home for him."

"Uumph," was the only response she received. She tried again. "How long has the child been with you?"

He frowned at her, as if it suddenly occurred to him that she was disturbing his peace. "A few months."

"And may I ask your name?"

"Salina, *señora;* and now, if you don't mind, I'd like to take a nap."

"Mr. Salina! You expect your nephew to work while you take a nap?"

Salina sighed heavily with displeasure and plopped his chair down on all four legs. Getting up, he started to brush past her, but her arm shot out to detain him.

"Wait a minute! What do you do in the cantina?"

"I am the cook, *señora.*" And with that, he lumbered past her.

Lisa stood there a moment longer, indecision written in every line of her body, until she heard Salina yelling at Patricio. She had the screen door halfway open before she made herself stop and think. Damn it! What did she think she was doing? More importantly, what did she think she *could* do?

Turning on her heel, she walked determinedly away, silently cursing the man-drawn line that divided two countries and that made such a difference in their standards of living. And after all, she tried to reason with herself between curses, it was none of her business. What did she know of the matter, when it came right down to it? She was a visitor in a foreign country for just a short time, and she would do well to remember the fact.

Engrossed in these thoughts, she didn't realize that Christopher was waiting for her, until she had nearly reached the cabin. And, so, his "Good morning, where have you been?" startled her.

"Oh, hi," she returned, unable to determine how she felt about finding him waiting for her. She resorted to generalities. "I've just been for a walk. It's a beautiful day."

"True." He smiled at her, making her come to an abrupt halt a few feet away. She didn't like the way his smile made her feel. Hell, she thought, gnawing on her bottom lip. This whole damn situation was fast becoming too awkward for her to handle. A divorced couple meeting on the same beach where they had honeymooned six years before. It was preposterous. If she ever had a spare moment, it might be interesting to find out what the books on etiquette said about such a situation.

"Is anything wrong?" he asked, strolling toward her.

Unknowingly, she scowled at him. "No, of course not. What could be wrong?"

Hands on his hips, he stared at her for a moment, then shrugged. "Nothing, I suppose. Have you had breakfast yet? I saw you coming from the cantina."

"No, I guess I forgot about breakfast this morning."

"Lisa, what's the matter with you? You sound as if your mind is a hundred miles away."

She shook her head, not willing to admit that her mind had been on him all morning. And now added to that was a little boy named Patricio. "I'm sorry. I guess I'm just tired. I think I'll go in and lie down for a while."

Christopher eyed her consideringly. "Would you like to go into town later?"

"I don't think so. You go ahead, though. Maybe I'll see you later." She favored him with a quick almost-smile and walked up the steps into the cabin.

Well, that's that, she thought as she turned and watched him stroll down the track toward the cantina. If he thought she was going to spend her entire vacation with him, he was sadly mistaken. She had come down here to be alone and to have time to think, and, Christopher Saxon or no Christopher Saxon, that was exactly what she intended to do.

In the end, she found that she was simply too tense to lie down. She did a few chores around the cabin, changed into coral-colored shorts and a matching sun top, and then headed down to the beach.

*   *   *

Lisa had lost all track of time and couldn't remember how long she had been lying on the beach. Dipping and wheeling above her, the sea gulls mocked her faint effort to recall the time. They were right, she decided with a contented wiggle, burrowing her towel more deeply into the sand with the motion. It didn't matter.

The mood of Baja had reached into her, converting her to its philosophy of tranquillity. Beyond her the muted rumble of the ocean provided a lullaby, against which she was finally beginning to let go of some of her tension. The warm, moist air rippled in soothing streams over her and wound through her auburn curls with gentle and intricate care; the sunshine coated her body with a saffron layer of warmth that went bone deep; and beneath her, the fine sand conformed to her shape and cushioned her on its pliant bed.

"You're going to burn." The deep voice immediately erased all the good that had been accomplished in the last couple of hours.

Rolling over, she shaded her eyes against the glare. "No, I'm not. I've used a sunscreen."

Christopher dropped down uninvited beside her. Wearing only a pair of brief shorts, he was quintessentially male. Hair lay over his legs, arms, and chest in compelling drifts of golden brown that unaccountably made her want to reach out and stroke them. He had the type of skin that allowed him never to worry about burning, and Lisa tingled with warmth as she watched how his well-developed muscles flexed under the taut, smooth skin as he settled on one elbow and looked down at her.

"Have you been in yet?" he questioned, indicating the tumbling blue waves that fell into kaleidoscopic spider webs not far from their feet.

She shook her head. "I didn't even bring a swimsuit with me. I figured the water would still be too cold. Besides, if you'll remember, I'm not that strong a swimmer."

"I'll take you in if you like. You don't really need a suit. There's no one on the beach but us."

Words that should have been spoken died in her throat. The heat of his body reached out to her, penetrating her skin without him even coming into contact with her. Misting in on a soft zephyr, the tangy scent of the sea blended with the musky smell of Christopher, merging into her senses with a subtle intoxication. A soft languor diffused her body, and with it, her defenses against him were weakened.

"You've grown more beautiful, Lisa."

His deep voice rolled through her with the force of a blow to her stomach. He left her speechless. He left her breathless.

"I was never beautiful," she repudiated on a thread of a sound. "You only thought I was."

"Yes," he agreed softly. "I thought you were. I still do."

Without warning, his fingers teased across her midriff, lightly brushing grains of sand off her bare flesh. She stiffened. Even taking last night into account, it was incredible that, after four years of being apart, this feeling of instant intimacy could still spring up between them.

"You were something as a young girl," he whispered, "but you've matured into an extraordinary woman, Lisa."

His hand rubbed back and forth under her suddenly aching breasts. Helplessly, she could feel them swelling against the cloth of her halter-necked top. It had been so long since he had held their soft weight in his hands. Last night he had only touched them through her dress. Traitorously, her mind supported her body's need to feel his hands against her by recalling vividly the feelings he had always been able to evoke by taking her naked breast in his hand.

Christopher's hand stilled as if he had just heard her thoughts, and Lisa forced herself to wipe her mind clear.

It must have worked. His hand slid away from her chest. However, the area to which it moved wasn't much better for her peace of mind. Down past the waistband of her shorts, his fingers spread nearly the width of her belly. "You've always had a flat stomach, but now"—his hand slipped over her side—"your hips have developed the most enchanting roundness. They make a man want to curl his hands around them."

"Christopher . . ." His name, which had started out as a warning, disintegrated into a moan when he did just that, briefly cupping one buttock and squeezing.

"And your legs"—his hand continued on its journey of discovery, down the outside of her thighs, pushing a liquid sweetness through her bloodstream as it went—"seem even longer."

"Christopher, don't."

He didn't seem to hear her protest. Maybe the roar of the ocean was too loud—or *maybe* her protest was too soft.

His fingers feathered to the tender inside of her thigh, and, without even being aware of it, she opened her legs a little wider. Tracing a straight line until he reached her shorts, he stopped and pressed his strong fingers softly into the silky curves.

"It's not over with us, Lisa. Not by a long shot. I can still make your body quiver under my hands, and you can still make me want to bury myself deep inside you and never leave."

"No." Her head shook back and forth in denial, while her treacherous body clamored voraciously for more.

"We only had to see each other for it to start again. Admit it."

His fingers kneaded up into her through the material of her shorts, causing a hard shock of heat to hit her system like a blow.

"No . . . no . . . oh, God, yes."

He laughed softly, and, leaving that vulnerable part of her body, his hand drew up the outside of her torso to the sides of her breasts. There his thumbs reached to circle the hard outline of her nipples against the thin cotton.

Lisa's brain ceased to operate for just a moment, and when it became functional again, her top was off and lying on the sand beside her.

Rolling the rigid peak of her breast around with his tongue, Christopher muttered hoarsely, "God, Lisa, do you have any idea how good you taste? There's not another taste like you in the whole world. I'm convinced, the flavor of you is unique." He settled on top of her, and she could feel his pulsing hardness pressing erotically into the lower portion of her answering body. "I want to kiss you all over."

He licked and nibbled around the soft skin of her breasts, taking them in his hands and moving them into the path of his mouth. Radiant sunshine and the velvet moistness of Christopher's tongue tingled over her hot flesh, and the feelings intermingled in her mind. It all felt so good and she wanted to absorb more, so much more. And yet she knew there was something vaguely wrong with that feeling.

"Christopher," she gasped, somehow realizing that she was coming very close to crossing that line where she would lose all control, and that she hadn't fully thought this whole thing out yet. "This isn't reasonable. . . ."

"What's reasonable? You want this as much as I do."

"No! You're wrong," she cried out in desperation, as much to get through to herself as to get through to him. "M-maybe it's easy to give into the feelings of the moment, but what's not so easy is to forget the pain I felt four years ago when you left me."

He stilled. Silently, he raised his head. His breathing was harsh. He gave no clue as to what he was thinking, but Lisa knew she finally had his full attention, so she continued.

"Do you know what I had to do to get used to sleeping alone? I would put pillows all around me so that in the night I could feel something warm against me and pretend it was you."

"You don't think I had that same pain, Lisa?"

"I don't know. You're the one who made the decision to leave."

"And it never occurred to you that I was trying to give us both time to stop the self-destructive merry-go-round we had somehow climbed on?"

"It might have if you had said something."

"Maybe I would have if you hadn't gone running back to Daddy so fast and he hadn't been so quick with that damned lawyer of his." He sighed heavily and sat up. "Look, we both acted pretty rashly four years ago, but maybe we should give ourselves another chance now."

"For what purpose?"

He watched while she reached for her top and fastened it around her with trembling hands. "I think I've just shown the purpose," he said.

"Sex?" she scoffed.

"It's there. We can't ignore it."

"Watch me," she suggested with more force than she felt.

"There might be something more than sex left, if we're willing to look."

"It doesn't matter. I'm not willing to risk that pain again."

"I'm not talking about pain, Lisa."

"Yes, you are."

"No, honey, I'm not. I'm talking about us spending time together. We can take it slowly."

A shiver of remembrance coursed through her at his easy use of the familiar endearment. "That's what you said when you first mentioned the idea, and I don't know about you, but what just happened is *not* my idea of slow."

"Okay, I'll back off if it'll make you feel any better."

"I don't know, Christopher. I just don't know."

And yet when he asked her to dinner that night, she accepted. And when he came by the next morning and asked if she'd like to go for a walk on the beach, she went.

She had spoken the truth, though. She was totally confused about the issue of her and Christopher. But one thing she did know now, with absolute, rock-bottom certainty, was that she could not marry Robert. Not now. Not as long as her reactions to Christopher could be so easily and explosively inflamed.

*   *   *

It was just after dawn, the morning mist not yet burned away, when Lisa scrambled down the cliff. Patricio hadn't seen her. Standing ankle-deep in the surf, he cast far out on the water for his and his uncle's breakfast.

It had been quite by accident that Lisa had discovered Patricio's practice of fishing every morning. Five days ago, after a particularly sleepless night, she had been wandering the cliffs and spied him down below her about a mile south of the cabin.

Now she met him there every morning. It was her chance to get better acquainted with him, without the oppressive influence of his uncle, and they had become surprisingly close. Also, she acknowledged wryly, it was practically her only respite from the undercurrent of sexual tension that flowed back and forth between her and Christopher so effortlessly and so powerfully.

"Good morning, Patricio," she called when she was close enough for him to hear.

"Lisa!" His solemn face broke into an all-too-seldom-seen smile.

Every time she saw that smile, something fierce and indefinable clutched at her heart. She had known him less than a week, yet the feeling was strong, and was getting stronger.

"How are the fish biting this morning?"

"Not so good." The smile vanished. "Some days, the fish, they just have better things to do than bite at my hook."

The inherently sad tone of his voice made her question, "If you don't catch anything, what will you do for breakfast?"

He shrugged his thin shoulders. "I will wait for lunch."

Lisa was incensed. "Do you often go without meals?"

"Sometimes." He turned those liquid dark eyes of his on her. "Sometimes I go to sleep hungry, but a lot of people do."

"I bet your uncle doesn't," she muttered to herself.

"Señora?"

"Never mind." Lisa didn't notice that there was new resolve in her voice when she asked, "Does your uncle often mistreat you?"

However, she did take note of the fact that Patricio didn't answer her directly. "It is hard for him. He has always lived alone, and it is a big job to care for me. He only took me in because my mother, she was his sister."

Lisa shook her head in amazement. "How did you get to be so old, Patricio?"

He didn't misunderstand her. There was already a bond between the two of them. "My mother and I were alone for a long time before she died. I had to take care of her."

"What about your father?"

"I don't think I ever had one," he stated with an adult air of acceptance out of place in one so young.

It was hard to say just when the shadow of the idea had entered her mind. Perhaps when she had first looked into those meltingly sad eyes. But now the idea was there, crystallized, passionate, and full-blown. Why not?

She had always wanted a child, but the two years of her marriage to Christopher had been so turbulent, it had never seemed the right time. And then there had been no more marriage left. And there was the very distinct possibility that she might never remarry. But she had her career and now she was determined to have Patricio.

"Patricio, do you trust me?"

"*Sí, señora. Por supuesto.*"

"Would you like to come live with me, in the United States?"

"*Es posible?*"

"I don't see why not. Your uncle certainly—well, as you said, it's a big job for him to care for you. But I'll have to go into town and contact a lawyer. He'll tell me how to proceed."

"You mean I could come live with you?" he asked uncertainly.

Her heart melted. "Yes, Patricio, you could come live with me and be my little boy."

"You promise?"

"I promise."

Four

Christopher never insisted that they spend time together. Instead, he just seemed to show up, suggest something, and they would do it. It was so simple. Lisa hadn't yet been able to figure out how he managed to manipulate her so adroitly.

Today had been no exception, she reflected moodily as she viewed Christopher, her blue eyes narrowed against the festive light of the day. Lounging across the table from her at a small outdoor café, he was at his most dangerous, as he exerted every effort to be charming.

The decor of Ensenada, the third largest city in Baja and the leading seaport, classically easygoing and splendidly cheerful, was their backdrop. There wasn't a cloud in sight.

But Lisa had become increasingly unsettled as the day wore on. They had shopped all morning, looking at flawlessly designed jewelry, finely wrought art objects, and a myriad of leather goods.

Giving the matter some consideration, Lisa decided that maybe it wasn't so much the shopping that had bothered her as much as *how* Christopher shopped.

"I liked that cape you tried on." His deep voice inserted itself into her thoughts. "Do you want to go back and buy it after we've finished eating?"

The leather cape. When he had wrapped it around her shoulders from behind, his hands had lingered and she had been able to feel his warm breath against the side of her neck as he leaned around to fasten the hook.

"No. I think it's too heavy for our climate. I doubt if it would ever get cold enough for me to wear it."

"You're probably right. It's too bad. Well, what about the necklace? I thought it looked beautiful on you."

The necklace. When he had held up the silver filigree necklace to her throat, his fingers had brushed softly against the curves that swelled under her T-shirt. Her nipples had hardened instantly and visibly, and his gaze had touched them with an erotic impact that had made her gasp.

"N-no. I think it was a little too elaborate for my taste."

What kind of defenses was she supposed to put up against a man like her ex-husband? It seemed so easy for him to cause these honeyed feelings to disperse to every corner of her body—just by a casual look or a chance touch. What was the answer?

Lisa felt the tightening in her stomach that had been with her for quite some time, and which made eating nearly impossible. She finally gave up and reached for her margarita. After taking a sip, she said, "Tell me about this lady you've been seeing."

Surprise made Christopher's eyebrows arch. Surprise at her own daring made Lisa's stomach tighten even more, and she took another drink of the cool, salty liquid, feeling it slide down her throat and tangle with the hard knot in her stomach. It didn't help. Neither did Christopher's words.

"Catherine is a lovely woman. She was widowed about a year before I met her."

Lisa licked some salt off her upper lip and made an effort to keep her voice steady. "I see. How long have you known her?"

"A couple of years. We've helped each other through some bad times."

Lisa couldn't seem to keep the sarcasm out of her response. "How nice for you." She had had no one to help her through the bad times. The only solace had been her studies. "Are you going to marry her?"

Christopher pulled out a cigarette and lit it, exhaling the smoke in a screen around him before he answered. "As I told you, I've thought about it."

Where her courage was coming from she didn't know, but she swallowed hard and asked, "And how close are you to making a decision?"

"I've made it." His green eyes appeared opaque, impossible to read.

Lisa looked away from him, all courage instantly deserting her. She wasn't going to ask what his decision was, because she had a terrible feeling it would hurt too much.

The next evening they dined at a restaurant on the water's edge, enjoying succulent lobster with almonds and a white wine sauce and an incomparable view of the sunset. With the darkness came a strolling band of mariachis, but the ambience was lost on Lisa.

There was only Christopher. His green eyes, with their mysterious depths, were sparkling at her. His lips were smiling at her, their sensual fullness parted in tender humor.

It all seemed to come so naturally to him—looking and smiling at her in that bedeviling way. He didn't seem to be torn apart by the doubts and confusion she was suffering from. He didn't seem to notice the way her body reacted to his while they were still feet or even yards apart.

She jumped, suddenly aware that he was speaking to her. "I beg your pardon?"

"Am I boring you, Lisa?" he questioned with a teasing smile that made her lungs gasp for air.

Boring? He had to be joking! "No, not at all,"

she returned with what she hoped was at least a reasonable facsimile of utter calm. "I'm afraid my mind just drifted away for a moment."

"Where to?" The question came softly.

"No place a man like you would find interesting, I'm sure."

"Try me."

Damn! He was doing it to her again. Backing her into a corner with just a word or an inflection of his voice. She *had* to stop reacting to him like this. It was ludicrous. Surely ex-husbands weren't supposed to affect a person like this. Were they?

"Suppose we get back to what you were saying," she suggested lamely.

His expression mocked her for a moment, but his voice betrayed how serious he was. "I was saying how much I love this place."

"Really?"

"Yeah. Baja is one of the few places I've ever found where I can relax completely. It's so peaceful. Don't you think?"

Peaceful? She gulped. "Yes, it's quite lovely."

"I've been down here quite a few times in the last four years."

Alone? she wondered. Aloud, she asked, "Where did you stay?"

"I stayed at the hotel once and at the Monroes' the rest of the time. I've been seriously considering buying my own place."

"Oh? Have you done any looking?"

"Some." He shrugged. "But I haven't found

anything. What I'd really like to do is design my own house. That's what I did for my place in the canyon in Valencia."

"I didn't know that." For some reason, this conversation had become very painful. It just didn't seem right that Christopher should be doing and planning these things without her. But what really didn't seem right was that the thought of him doing these things should hurt her so.

Lisa watched while Christopher's long fingers absently stroked the bowl of the wineglass in front of him.

"I know what I want. It's just a matter of finding it or the right location to build on."

"What exactly are you looking for?"

"Absolute privacy, with every room having an unobstructed view of the ocean."

"I find it hard to picture you relaxing, Christopher. You never used to be able to."

He carried his wineglass to his lips and took a long drink. Lisa followed the progress of the wine down his throat as the strong column moved in the swallowing motion.

Some moisture remained on his lips, but he didn't seem to notice as he said, "Presumably, with age comes wisdom, and I've learned a thing or two about myself. I work very hard with my mind. There are times when I need the luxury of *not* thinking, of feeling the wind blow against my face and of watching the mesmerizing changes of color and light on the ocean and letting them play in my mind."

Lisa stared at him, fascinated. Had she ever really known Christopher? Or had he changed so much? It was possible. She certainly felt as if she had undergone great changes in the last four years.

Later, driving home, they met very few other cars on the narrow two-lane road. The intimacy of the night enclosed them, isolating them in the luxuriant closeness of the car, with the drone of the powerful engine the only sound in the still night. And then when he stopped the car beside the cabin and turned off the engine, there was only the quiet sound of their breathing left.

He turned in his seat to face her, just looking at her. His face was in partial darkness, and she couldn't see his expression. But she knew he was watching her, and she held her breath for what would come next. She knew he would take her in his arms and kiss her, and she also knew that she wanted him to . . . very much.

But with an unforeseen motion, he leaned across the car and opened her door for her. "I'll see you around, Lisa."

With automatic movements, she climbed out and walked to the door, stunned. He waited until she was safely inside, then started his engine and gunned off down the track.

And far into the night, Lisa lay awake, her body discontent with unsatisfied . . . questions.

*　　*　　*

Lisa eyed Señor Salina with genuine dislike. The lawyer had told her that she could not take Patricio back with her until the adoption was final, even if immigration papers were issued.

She hated leaving Patricio with his uncle for one more day than she needed to, but there didn't seem to be any alternative.

"I've given my lawyer, Señor Martinez, your name, and he will be in touch with you. I'd appreciate your cooperating with him."

Salina's eyes were narrowed with concentration as he stared at her. "I don't know, *señora.* Patricio, he's my flesh and blood. I'm not sure my sister would like the idea of an *Americana* adopting him."

"You know as well as I do, Señor Salina, that your sister would be thrilled that Patricio is going to have a home and someone who loves him."

"Still . . . I need the boy to help me in the cantina."

"I told you I'll be giving you a large sum of money. I'm sure it will more than make up for the loss of the boy. Now, I don't know how long all this will take, but I'm going to leave you money that should be more than enough to care for Patricio until I can come get him." Her voice hardened. "If I find that Patricio has been mistreated during this time, I promise you, Señor Salina, I will make you more than sorry."

Lisa squirmed on the opened sleeping bag she had spread out a few feet from the edge of the cliff. Trying to sunbathe was proving impossible. Her nerves were on a razor's edge. It had been three days since she and Christopher had returned from Ensenada. It had been a day and a half since they had had dinner. She hadn't seen him since.

What could he be doing? She hadn't heard his car go by. She jumped to her feet and smoothed her moist hands down her thighs. Maybe she would walk down to his little blue house and see if he wanted to do something. Since the beginning of their joint vacation, she hadn't sought him out. He had always been the one to come to her. Yet today she was uncommonly restless, her nerves stretched nearly to the breaking point, and not even her morning meetings with Patricio had been enough to divert her after they had parted.

Not even bothering to change into jeans, she set out down the track. No sound of any other humans reached her ears. Even though the population of the small community had expanded over the weekend, it appeared that they had all gone back to the States for the week. She and Christopher must be the only two people left on this stretch, she mused idly as she rounded the corner of his house.

The back of the house, the part that faced the ocean, was actually the front, and her foot was one step up the porch before she noticed Christopher. Utter shock held her motionless.

Apparently the two of them had had the same idea, but obviously he was having more luck at it than she had. He seemed to be having no trouble relaxing, as his powerful body lay dozing in the afternoon sun. And there was another difference, too. A difference that nearly stopped her heart from beating. *Christopher was completely naked.*

Lisa couldn't tear her gaze from the impressive and gut-wrenching picture he made. The brightness of the sun spotlighted the steel ropes of muscle just under his sweat-sheened skin. Merely looking at him made the ever-present knot in her stomach tighten, and her hand reached out for the support of the wooden post that helped frame the porch. A powerful ache began to throb deep in her loins as she watched him.

He was lying on his stomach, his face cradled on his arms and turned away from her. Off the ocean came a gentle gust of wind. It whispered across the hard contours of his body, following its lean line with loving concentration. When it reached his tightly muscled buttocks, it rustled ever so slightly through the tiny golden brown hairs that covered his skin, before continuing down his long, sinewy legs.

A flush of heat overcame Lisa, so intense that she suddenly felt as if the sun had become lodged inside of her. Longing, fierce and thick, struck her like a torrential storm hurtling out of the Pacific. A pulse pounded in her temple. It was minutes before she realized that her fingers had slid over the post and were caressing the weather-smoothed wood. Horrified to discover what she was doing, she looked at her hand. It was trembling.

With rigid determination, she turned, and by concentrating on the effort it took to put one foot in front of the other, she made it back to the cabin.

Too hot to sunbathe, too restless to take a nap, Lisa wrapped her arms around herself and paced the rest of the afternoon away, until finally, collapsing on the sofa, she fell into an uneasy sleep.

When she awoke, it was after dark. And she felt . . . prickly . . . itchy . . . hungry. But when she tried to eat, she found she couldn't.

Maybe a shower would make her feel better, she decided, a little desperately. But once there, she found that somehow it wasn't quite what she needed. The sun-heated water frothed over her body, tingling against her skin like a hundred gentle fingers. She shampooed her hair until her scalp hurt, then resignedly pulled the cord again to allow the crystalline liquid to pour over her, with its heated friction.

At last, dripping wet and wound up tighter than a mainspring, she retreated to the cabin. In the bedroom she dried off, roughly rubbing her skin with a thick terry towel, then slapping perfumed body lotion on every square inch of her.

Frowning darkly at the dress Christopher had bought her, she stepped into a pair of narrow panties. She looked at the dress again. Oh, what the hell. The dress was cool, swinging away from her body just under her breasts, and that was what counted at this point. Throwing it over her head, she zipped it up.

Now what? She chewed on her bottom lip and looked around indecisively. There was no place she wanted to go. And she wasn't hungry. There were at least a hundred paperback books in the cabin, but she had no desire to read any of them. She walked into the main room and looked around. She wanted . . . She closed her eyes for a moment. Oh, damn! *What did she want?*

She suddenly felt like screaming. *It was so stuffy in here.* She was suffocating. She had to get out!

Escaping out the door, she made her way to the edge of the cliff and drew a deep, uneven breath. A magnificent living painting, priceless and rare, greeted her. It was a spectacular sight that a person, if he was very lucky, might get to see once in a lifetime, and she stretched out on the sleeping bag to get a better look.

The night sky was a bolt of black velvet, deep and mysterious, perfect and cloudless and sequined with a million stars. A jeweled half-moon clasped the edge of the sky, and Lisa thought she had never seen anything more beautiful. It was vividly clear, without the lights from a city to obscure the blinding radiance that had been naturally created.

The night air felt cool against her fevered skin, and Lisa threw her arms over her head and shut her eyes in an attempt to let the unbounded tranquillity of the shining night enter her.

But her restive body wasn't cooperating. There was a hurting pressure in the lower portion of her body that refused to give her rest. An inarticulate moan escaped her lips, and her hips moved in a slight arch in an attempt to ease the heavy ache. It didn't help.

She turned her head from side to side in frustration. The aching went bone-deep. She ran her hands down to her stomach and pressed on the throbbing emptiness. What in the world was wrong with her?

Then she opened her eyes and suddenly he was there. Standing over her, larger than life, his feet straddling her legs, his hands on his hips, juxtapositioned against the star-spangled sky. He wore only jeans. His chest and feet were bare.

Now she knew what had been wrong with her the last day or two. What was *still* wrong with her. It was oh, so complicated. It was oh, so simple. *She was nearly sick with her need for Christopher.*

He dropped silently to his knees over her, then leaned down and grasped her wrists, holding them over her head.

The words "I love you" formed in her mind, but his mouth came down on hers and all coherency dissolved. Willingly she opened her mouth, and his tongue rammed into it, probing deeply, drinking her sweet essence hungrily. His hands aroused her in ceaseless hypnotic designs; his mouth enraptured her.

Then, in a motion at once leisurely and mind-spinning, he rolled her over, and she was lying on top of him. His hands slowly released the long zipper of her dress, and he trailed the tips of his fingers down the exposed curve of her spine, drawing a low moan from her. From head to toe, she melted into him.

Easing the soft blue garment off her shoulders in a whisper of a movement, he let it fall around her waist. He pulled her higher over him and his hot mouth found the tightened peak of her breast and sucked hungrily, as if he were dry and the taste of her could fill him up.

Raw need exploded in her stomach. He was swelled thick and hard against her, and she moved instinctively over him. His hands slipped along her thighs and under her dress, where his fingers dug into her buttocks and pulled her roughly against him.

Sensation followed dazzling sensation, until he groaned and rolled her over and she was again lying on her back with him beside her. It all seemed so very familiar. It all seemed so very right.

She hardly had time to breathe, before tiny kisses were being dropped on her eyes, her nose, her cheeks, her chin, her jawline, and his hand was pushing the dress farther down her body so that his fingers could find their way inside the low waistband of her panties.

The silver-and-black night seemed timeless. Below them the waves threw a crocheted shawl of white sparkling foam onto the beach. Beyond them the sea put on a light show of its own, phosphorescent-tipped waves that beamed shimmering life up into the velvet depths of space. Above them the stars rained their white-hot fire over them.

And Lisa felt drenched in a wild, incredible, fiery passion. She kicked aside her dress, raising her hips against his long fingers as they rubbed so intimately and knowledgeably against her. At the same time his mouth was moving back to her breast, licking, caressing, biting, driving her exquisitely crazy. A harsh shudder racked her body.

Christopher drew back, his eyes blazingly green and holding her spellbound in the black magic of the night. "Are you cold?" he questioned hoarsely.

"No . . . I'm *hot*." Her graphic words and her pulsating body left him in no doubt.

"*God!*"

His jeans were quickly peeled off, as was the remaining piece of silk that covered her. And then he was on her and in her. He filled her, he surrounded her, he engulfed her.

The earth spun on its axis, rocketing with maddening speed through the galaxy, and Christopher pressed into her, harder and harder, the pounding rhythm of the ocean at high tide an elemental background for their lovemaking.

Her hands were clenched in his hair and her breath was coming in short gasps. It was like nothing she had ever experienced before. Four years alone had made them incredibly hungry for each other, and they took their fill.

Their passion built, rising toward the heavens until it crested, blossoming among the stars and at last bursting apart and spraying out bits of brilliance to the farthest reaches of the black universe.

Then at last a stardust of finely crushed diamonds drifted down and covered them, and Lisa fell asleep in the arms of her ex-husband.

Five

Lisa fell asleep on the cliff, but she awoke in the upstairs bedroom of the cabin, alone. She lay perfectly still, feeling very much like a jigsaw puzzle that had been completed but now had all its pieces scattered to the four corners of the world. Her world. Her carefully planned world had come tumbling down last night.

She had come to Baja with the original intent of putting away the past once and for all, so that she could concentrate on her future. She had thought herself so smart to think of it. It had seemed so easy.

Now, remembering her thoughts right before Christopher's mouth had covered hers, she found herself considering the very real possibility that she might still be in love with her ex-husband. She groaned in distress. *It just couldn't be!* Her mind, which she had trained so well in the last few years, refused to accept this new informa-

74

tion, unable to adapt so quickly to this startling revelation.

Not only that, but she was about to become the mother of a seven-year-old boy. Talk about complications!

What had happened? Where had she gone wrong? She had turned around and looked up and seen Christopher on the cliff. Not smart, Lisa.

She had reached out to help a child and looked into liquid dark eyes of a seven-year-old boy already aged beyond his years. Not easy, Lisa.

She hadn't been able to resist either one of them. Not for the first time, she had to ask herself, *now what?*

For quite some time Lisa had been aware that muffled noises were coming from the kitchen. It could be mice, she thought hopefully. There were plenty of them around. It could even be someone who had broken in during the night and was helping himself to whatever he could find, she mused, deciding that that was probably her second-best bet. Lisa gave an inward sigh. Oh, hell. The way her luck was running, it was more than likely Christopher.

Sure enough, preceded by the rattle of cups and the aroma of coffee, he entered the room.

"Good morning," he said cheerfully, depositing a tray with two cups of coffee beside her.

She wrapped the sheet around her and sat up. "Is it?" The upstairs bedroom in the trailer didn't have an outside window.

"It sure is." He picked up a cup and handed it to her. "Here you are, just the way you like it, half coffee and half milk."

She peered into the cup with amazement. She had always taken her coffee that way because, even though she needed the caffeine to wake her up, she hated the taste of coffee. "You remembered!"

"I remembered," he murmured. "I remember a lot of things." His green eyes were clear and deep this morning, searching the depths of hers. "Don't you?"

She lowered her eyes and took a sip of coffee. "No," she denied, with a tremor in her voice that would probably fool very few people, least of all someone who had once known her as well as Christopher had. "I don't like to remember."

"I didn't say I *liked* to remember. I just said I did." The early-morning huskiness of his voice was tinted with sardonic humor. "What would you like to do today?"

She stared down into her coffee cup. "I've decided to go back home today."

Lisa hadn't realized she was holding her breath until she heard his quiet, "Just like that?" and she exhaled.

It had been an unconscious decision, but now that it was out, it seemed like a wonderful idea.

"No, not just like that. It—it'll take a couple of hours to clean and get the cabin ready to close up, and then there's the packing and the. . . ."

He lifted her chin with his finger, so that she had to look at him. "What are you doing, Lisa?"

"I'm running," she freely admitted. "I'm running just as hard and just as fast as I can."

"Why?"

"Because I'm having a hard time dealing with what happened last night."

"What happened between us last night was beautiful." His voice was softly erotic. "What's so hard to deal with about that?"

"Christopher!" She set her coffee cup down on the nightstand, because her hands were trembling so badly she was in danger of spilling it. "Last night should never have happened. We're divorced!"

"The minister said, 'Let no man put asunder.' "

"Christopher!"

"You said that," he pointed out, and began playing with one shining auburn curl that lay by the side of her neck.

"Look." She licked her lips nervously and felt his fingers still as his attention switched. "W-we met down here purely by chance. We were swept up in the mood of the place. But we both have built lives that are apart from each other now."

He drew his hand away from her and fixed her with a steady gaze. "What do you want to do, Lisa? Go back to our respective lives and forget that we met down here? Go back and forget that last night ever happened? Can you do that, Lisa? Can you just go back home and pick up again without missing a beat?"

"What do you want from me, Christopher?" The anguished words were torn from her heart. "Do you want me to pay for the hurt I caused you? Is that it? Because if that's what's behind all this, let me tell you, I've paid. Do you know that when you left, I cried until I thought I didn't have a tear left in me? But then I'd start again."

He leaned back on his elbows, and his eyes narrowed. "I felt as if an eighteen-wheeler, fully loaded, had run over me when I was served with those divorce papers."

Feeling the tears in her eyes that threatened to spill over, she whispered, "Four years are gone. We'll never get them back."

"One thousand four hundred and sixty-one nights," he returned flatly.

Resolutely she blinked back the tears. "Alone."

"And quite empty."

Lisa looked at him, her vision blurring despite her efforts, and said very slowly, "I repeat. What do you want from me? How much do I have to pay before you'll be satisfied?"

He studied her from beneath thick golden-brown lashes. "I've never stopped wanting you, Lisa."

"Last night—"

"Only whetted my appetite for you."

"Damn you, Christopher! Damn you for walking back into my life and destroying my peace of mind."

"Did you have peace of mind, Lisa? Real peace of mind?"

His sharp question took her aback momentarily. The truth, if she thought about it, was that she hadn't had peace since the day Christopher had left. How could a person have any peace when you were separated from the person you had loved so much? It might have appeared as if she had, but hiding underneath the calm surface had always been great ripples of disturbance. "What difference does it make?" she asked wearily. "Just get out of here so I can get dressed and go home."

"And then what?"

"What do you mean?" she questioned warily.

"I want to see you again."

"It won't work, Christopher. I'm not sure that two people can bridge that much time and pain."

A poignant silence filled the room. Christopher sat up and reached for his cigarettes. Without looking at her, he inserted one between his lips and lit it. "I'd still like to see you when we both get back home."

He wanted her. That much had been established. And, heaven help her, she wanted him, too. But whether she could bear to see him simply on that basis she just didn't know.

He was watching her. Waiting. She ran her tongue over her bottom lip in a repeat of the gesture that gave only a hint of the tenseness she was feeling. "You're going to have to give me time to think about this, Christopher."

"Okay. I'll give you time." He suddenly smiled with alarming charm. "For a while."

* * *

Packing her car and closing up the cabin was relatively easy. Finding Patricio to say good-bye was not. She finally traced him to a patch of shade behind the cantina, where he was peeling potatoes.

He looked up and smiled at her. If she had had any doubts about the adoption, that smile of happiness on his face would have eliminated them. But she didn't. "Hi, Patricio. I've come to say good-bye." His small face fell, and she could almost read his thoughts. She knelt beside him and took his hand in hers. "It won't be for very long. I promise. You and I will just have to be patient while we get all this paper work done, but it will get done, and then we'll be together for always."

"For always? Really?"

"Yes. Now, I don't want you to be afraid," she said, thinking of the cultural shock he would have to go through. "I know it will be a big change from what you're used to, but you're very smart and we'll do it together."

"Will you come to get me, Lisa?"

"You bet."

"You won't forget?"

"No, Patricio." She gathered him in her arms for a final hug. "I won't forget."

She was back at work the next day. She'd toyed briefly with the idea of taking off another day and lounging around her apartment pool. But she had decided finally that the best thing would be to go to the office, get involved, and not allow herself time to ruminate. She hadn't been at her desk more than ten minutes before Robert strolled in.

"Lisa, darling, I'm so glad to see you're back early." He leaned across her desk to place a kiss on her cheek. "How was your vacation?"

"Fine, Robert, just fine," she declared with considerably more enthusiasm than she felt, as he settled in the chair opposite her. He was in his early forties but didn't look it. He was lean and fit, and the gray that was threaded through his brown hair only made him look more distinguished. "I see the office managed to make it through my absence without falling apart."

"Ah, but your presence was sorely missed by all, especially me." His sincerity came through the somewhat trite words.

Lisa looked down at the papers on her desk, copies of the papers she'd filed for Patricio's adoption. "Robert, there are some things I have to discuss with you, some decisions I've made."

"And I want to talk to you about them, too, darling, since they concern our future together, but I have a client due in about ten minutes. Let's have dinner tonight," he suggested.

Lisa could tell by his tone that Robert was very sure that her answer to his marriage proposal would be yes. And he had every right to expect that any woman would jump at the chance to marry him. He was quite a catch, after all. "Uh, I had planned on seeing my father tonight. What about lunch?"

"Sorry, I have a luncheon to attend." Robert's life ran on a rigid schedule. "We could meet for drinks around five if that's all right with you."

"Yes, that will be fine," Lisa agreed quickly. She wanted to let him know as soon as possible that she couldn't marry him. It was weighing heavily on her conscience.

"Fine." He stood up and glanced down at the papers. "Don't tell me they've already assigned you a case! At least they could have let you get a cup of coffee first."

"No . . . that is, they didn't. This is personal."

"Really?" His fingers came out and swiveled the papers to face him. "Mexican-adoption and U.S. immigration papers! My God, Lisa. What have you gotten yourself into?"

She calmly reached out and turned the papers back. "That's one of the things I wanted to tell you about, Robert, but you're too busy at the moment, so I'll explain this evening."

"Lisa, darling." Robert put his fists on the desk and bent toward her. "You know I love you, but I'm really too old to be thinking about starting a family. I realize this is something we've never discussed, but perhaps we'd better take a moment and do so."

"Patricio is a seven-year-old boy who needs me, Robert. And probably the strangest part of this whole thing is that I need him too. I grew to love him in an incredibly short time, and just as soon as the law will allow, I'm bringing him back to live with me."

"He's Mexican?"

"That bothers you?"

"No, no, of course not." Lisa believed him. Robert was a genuinely nice person. "But a child just wouldn't fit into our lives at this stage of the game. I envisioned travel and lots of leisure time for us."

"Robert," she said gently. "I wasn't going to tell you until this evening, but I had already decided that marriage wouldn't work out between us."

He pushed himself away from the desk. "But why? This thing about the child can be worked out, Lisa. I'm sure that once we discuss it, we can come to some compromise. Don't let the matter of the boy come between us."

"It's not that." She hesitated, trying to find the right words. "You see, by some quirk of fate, Christopher was down in Baja, too."

"At the cabin?"

Lisa repressed a smile. Robert's sense of propriety was clearly outraged. "No. He was staying down the track at another house. But . . . well, we saw quite a bit of each other while we were there, and . . . I've found I still have some feelings for him."

Robert sank back into the chair. "Are you saying that you're still in *love* with him?"

She nervously rejected the idea. "I'm saying that there is still something very strong between Christopher and me. Everything has happened so fast, I haven't been able to sort it all out yet. But I know that I can't marry you."

"Are you sure, Lisa? Are you one hundred percent sure?"

She nodded silently.

"Damn it! I knew you shouldn't have gone down there by yourself."

"I'm glad I did, Robert. Don't you see? When two people talk about marriage, they should be very, very certain. I failed the first time. I have no intention of making a failure out of another marriage."

He regarded her soberly. "Then, you and Christopher have discussed the possibility of remarriage?"

"Good heavens, no!" Levering herself up from the chair, she paced to the window. "Two wrongs don't make a right."

"But you just said that there's still something very strong between the two of you."

"Right." She gave him a sad smile over her shoulder. "There is. I can't begin to read Christopher, so admittedly I don't know what he's thinking, yet I doubt very seriously if it's love he feels for me after all this time."

Robert came up behind her and turned her around. "I'm not sure I believe that, Lisa, but I'm not about to argue your ex-husband's case with you. For now, just know that I'm here for you if you need me."

"Thank you, Robert. That's very sweet of you."

"Not sweet at all. Just practical. Maybe one day you'll open your eyes and see me, instead of him."

The home Lisa had grown up in could best be described as stately and formal. Those same words could also be used to describe her father.

He was a banker, and a man completely devoted to convention and habit. Change came very hard to him, but in the last few years, age had forced certain alterations in his way of life. One was that he no longer worked the twelve-to-sixteen-hour days he had when he was younger. Then, too, he seemed less absolute in his views, more willing to listen to others.

Yet some things never changed. Her mother had died when Lisa was fourteen years old, and Lisa had left home six years later, but her father still lived on alone in the huge house. Dinner was still at seven, and Jane, the pleasant woman who had been their housekeeper for longer than Lisa could remember, still served it in the formal dining room.

Lisa glanced across the gleaming mahogany table at her father. "You really ought to take Uncle William up on his offer to go with him to the cabin one of these days. I think you'd enjoy it."

"I've lived this long without going down there, and I think I'll continue to do so. I have never been able to understand Baja's attraction for you people."

"That's because you've never been there," she chided gently.

"Perhaps. But tell me, how did you get on? Were you lonely? I worried about you."

Lisa was touched. Expressing emotion of any kind had always been hard for her father. She knew he hadn't been feeling well lately, and she decided it might be best not to mention that Christopher had showed up. However, there was someone she simply couldn't put off telling him about.

"I never got a chance to be lonely," she remarked honestly. "Father, I met the most wonderful little boy down there."

"Little boy? Since when have you taken to associating with children, Lisa?"

"Patricio is so special, Father. He's seven and has no parents, only an uncle who has no use for him other than what work he can get out of him."

Her father paused in the act of sipping a drink of water. "Are you saying that the child is being mistreated?"

"That's exactly what I'm saying."

"Surely there are agencies or organizations down there that can help. Did you look into it?"

"Actually, I did quite a bit more than that, Father. I've started adoption proceedings."

Her father abruptly lowered his crystal water goblet to the table. "Lisa! You can't be serious!"

"I'm very serious, Father. Patricio needs someone to care for him and about him. I can do that easily."

"But have you really thought about this? A child

will cause a drastic change in your life-style. And the problems of a single mother can be staggering."

"Don't worry." She smiled. "We'll be fine. Patricio and I will help each other."

"It will be a terrible cultural shock to the boy." He shook his head. "Language, style of life. I can foresee any number of problems."

"I never said it would be easy. But if you could see Patricio, Father, you would understand why I want to do this."

Her father got a faraway look in his eyes. "You know, when you were growing up, I never spent much time with you. I always thought I could make it up to you, but I don't think I ever really did. And then I thought, well, perhaps when Lisa has children. But I'm afraid I botched that up too."

"Father, you did no such thing. Christopher and I were quite good at ruining our marriage all by ourselves."

"Nevertheless, I wasn't a help. Once you married Christopher, I should have given more support. I've come to regret my negative attitude very much in the past few years."

"Oh, Father, please don't concern yourself." Lisa reached for his hand. "I'm fine."

"Maybe." He looked at her with his still-shrewd eyes. "Maybe. But if I can be of any help with Patricio, I don't want you to hesitate to come to me. Do you hear me?"

"Yes, I hear you," Lisa said, fighting the tears in her eyes. "And thank you, Father. You'll never know how much your saying these things means to me."

Six

One morning after Lisa had been back about a week, Robert appeared in her office with a rather bemused expression, an expression that didn't appear often on his distinguished face. "I just got a telephone call requesting your services."

"Oh? Is there some problem? You don't look particularly happy about it."

"I'm not," he admitted ruefully as he sat down opposite her and crossed his legs. "Even though I realize I'm in no position to object to anything you do."

"Robert"—her brow creased with perplexity—"you're the senior partner of this firm. Of course you have a right."

"I don't mean professionally. I mean personally," he stated quietly.

"Oh, Robert." She sighed. "I'm so genuinely sorry. You know I never meant to hurt you."

He held up his hand. "I know that. You've been

very up front with me about your feelings for Christopher, and even though it wasn't what I wanted to hear, I've appreciated your honesty. That's not the problem."

"So what is?"

"The telephone call was from him."

"Who?" She had lost the thread of the conversation.

"Your ex-husband."

"Christopher! Christopher called you?" At Robert's affirmative nod, she asked, "But why?"

"He wants your legal expertise to help him with some new electronic product that he has developed."

"Oh, yes, the chip," she murmured dazedly.

"I guess. At any rate, he claims it would take quite a bit of time and that you would probably have to stay up there."

"Up there?"

"I believe his corporation is located in Valencia, which is in the Santa Clarita Valley. From what I can gather, it's quite a growing concern. I took the liberty of making a few inquiries, and from all accounts Saxon Electronics is already astoundingly successful, and its future seems unlimited. Even now the industry is paying attention to it, watching it for indications of trends. I suppose, looking at it from a strictly objective viewpoint, it would be quite a feather in our firm's cap to get that account."

Lisa suddenly felt as if she were getting a headache. But that was impossible, because she never got headaches. "Robert, what did you tell him?"

"I told him it was up to you."

"Oh, great." Lisa slumped down in her chair and rested her now truly aching head in her hand.

"I also told him you would call him with your answer." Robert stood up and shoved a piece of paper toward her. "Here's his number. Let me know your decision."

Lisa stared at the number. What was Christopher doing? She had asked him for time to think. Evidently he thought a week was a sufficient amount of time. She smiled ruefully. He obviously didn't realize just how confused she was.

But several things had come out of the trip to Baja. Several things she could count on as hard fact. The first was that she now had a new and different view of the breakup of their marriage. She no longer looked at it in black-and-white terms. She had learned from their somewhat heated exchanges that there were all sorts of shades of gray in which a person could become entangled. She had come a long way, though. Four years ago she wouldn't have been able to consider the shades of gray and how one had to deal with them practically every day of one's life.

And, of course, there was the most astounding fact of all: the possibility that she still might be in love with Christopher.

Given all that, she had to wonder two things.

What was Christopher up to now, and what was her answer to him going to be?

Lisa went in search of two aspirin, took them, and then returned to her office. Picking up the phone, she dialed the number Robert had given her. A cheerful young man answered the phone with, "Saxon Electronics. What can we do for you?"

"Well, gee, I don't know. What are you offering?"

"Anything you want, ma'am," he came back quickly, unfazed by her retort. "In the field of electronics, that is. We're the best in the west."

"What about the east?"

"They don't count. Now, if you require anything that doesn't pertain to electronics but is of perhaps a more personal nature, I'm sure, given the sound of your lovely voice, that we can come to some mutual agreement."

Lisa howled with laughter. "My goodness! Are you allowed to answer the phone often?"

"Only when the secretary is out to lunch," he admitted a trifle sadly. "Or when everyone else is busy. Any other time, you will find me by the side of the great man himself."

"Great man?"

"Christopher Saxon. I'm his sort-of-assistant."

"I see. Well, I have a feeling I don't have time to delve into what exactly a 'sort-of-assistant' does. Do you think I could speak with him?"

"That depends. Perhaps if you told me what this is about, I could help you." The cheerful voice grew guarded. "Mr. Saxon is very busy and doesn't have time to talk to everyone."

"He'll talk to me. This is Lisa Saxon."

"Lisa Saxon," he repeated, as if he were writing it down. *"Lisa Saxon!* Uh, yes, ma'am. Just a moment, Mrs. Saxon."

The next voice she heard was her ex-husband's deeply disquieting one. "Lisa, it's nice to hear from you."

"Christopher, what's all this about my coming up there and working for you?" She cringed at the blustering way her words had come out. Hearing his voice for the first time in a week had disturbed her more than she had thought possible.

"Not interested in pleasantries, huh? Well, since you're so anxious to come straight to the point, let's have dinner tonight and I'll tell you all about it."

"Dinner?" She was definitely not conducting her side of this conversation with her usual aplomb or even intelligence, Lisa decided forlornly.

"Right. I'll drive over and pick you up at your apartment around eight."

"Eight?" Eight, she thought, let's see, if he picks me up at eight, I'll have to be home around six so that I can—

"Eight," he repeated. "I'll see you then. Good-bye."

"Good-bye?"

Lisa scowled at her reflection in the mirror. "You're twenty-seven years old," she told herself

bracingly. "And you're a lawyer. Think about tonight as if you were only going out to dinner with a
prospective client. You've done it many times
before, and you can handle this."

She twisted to get a better view of her turquoise
dress, which seemed to float away from her every
time she moved, then continued her monologue.
"There's no reason why the two of you can't have
a business relationship." Turning back, she criti-
cally eyed the most unbusinesslike way in which
the neckline of the sleeveless dress plunged to
show off her newly acquired tan, however slight.
"People do it all the time. You're a lawyer, for
heaven's sake," she reiterated. "A professional
woman. You can handle anything he throws at
you."

Swiveling, she scanned her bedroom for her
purse. "Just because the last time he saw you,
you were in bed, naked, after a night of his
lovemaking"—she scooped a comb out of the purse
and waved it at the mirror—"doesn't mean you
have to be apprehensive about seeing him again."
She flicked the comb through her tumbled curls,
and tossed it back in the purse just as the door-
bell rang.

Giving herself one last look, she repeated sternly,
"You're twenty-seven and a lawyer! Just keep reminding yourself of those two facts over and over
and you'll be fine. He's just someone who wants to
hire your services . . . your *legal* services," she

added as an afterthought, as if her image in the mirror had suggested differently.

She opened the door, and Christopher stood before her. He wore a beige silk shirt opened at the throat with the collar turned back over the lapels of a linen beige sports coat. His brown pants perfectly fitted his long, muscular thighs, and his hard face and bare throat were tanned, a tan she knew extended over his entire body.

She was in trouble!

She muttered, "Oh, God," and sagged against the door.

"No, it's just me." He smiled at her and strolled into her apartment.

"Christopher . . ." she began, wanting to suggest they go right out to the restaurant. For some reason, she didn't want him in her small apartment. The apartment she had lived in by herself for the last four years.

"Right. I was hoping you wouldn't forget." He stood in the center of her living room and looked around. "This is very nice."

"I'll probably be moving soon." She practically growled the words. It was true. She had already decided she would need a bigger place for Patricio. Most likely a house with a yard.

"Oh?" His eyebrows raised in inquiry. "Do you have anything particular in mind?" He crossed the room to finger the petals of the giant bouquet of paper flowers he had given her in Baja.

"No. Look, do you mind if we go? I'm really quite hungry."

"Of course," he agreed smoothly, moving to her before she had time to blink. "I can't have my lawyer starving, now, can I? But first *I* need to be fed."

And in another surprisingly fast action, his hands cradled the sides of her face. Then his mouth touched hers and his tongue parted her lips and the room no longer stood still. It spun, and she clung to him helplessly, her blood soaring with excitement. He moved his mouth over hers with a hot, wet, sensual passion. Her fingers dug deeply through the thick, vital texture of his hair, and she made no protest when his hands changed position and pulled her closer to him, fitting her softness to every hard muscle and bulge of him.

"You taste so sweet," he muttered, his lips running down her throat to rest against the sensitive skin that lay over the fiercely pounding pulse point. "So very sweet." He took her mouth again, kissing her until she was almost senseless.

"Oh, Christopher," she breathed.

"That's right, honey." He pulled back and laughed huskily. "Come on. Let's go feed you."

His green eyes were glowing with an inner light that made her uneasy, and Lisa wasn't at all sure it was wise to go with him. But she did.

And surprisingly, two hours later Lisa found herself totally relaxed and enjoying the evening.

Sitting across the dimly lit table from her ex-husband, she tried to decide how this had come about. It might have been because of the comfortably intimate atmosphere of the restaurant, or it might have been the soothing chilled wine. Then, too, there was the softly delicate beat of the guitars playing in the background to consider. But she knew it was because of the good-humored ease of Christopher himself. When he tried, he could be quite irresistible. Especially to someone, such as herself, who had *never* been able to resist him.

After kissing her at the apartment, he seemed to be deliberately backing off. He was charming in an entirely nonthreatening way, amusing her with anecdotes about his company and the bright young men and women who worked for him. He was disarming her because he wanted her to accept the temporary position of legal counsel for his company, and she knew it. But somehow she couldn't summon the strength to object.

The waiter placed their after-dinner coffee in front of them, a brandy too for Christopher. He waited until she had taken several sips of her coffee before he brought up the subject of working together.

"So, what do you think of the idea of coming to help me out for a while?"

"I really can't make a decision until I know more about it. I have a lot of questions."

He tilted his head toward her. "That's one of the reasons why we're here, honey. Ask away."

Briefly, she passed a hand over her eyes. She wished he wouldn't call her "honey." Each time he used that endearment, and so casually, too, it created a hopeless longing in her for the time when he had been as much in love with her as she had been with him.

"Okay," she said, more sharply than she'd intended. "What exactly are we talking about?"

His eyes narrowed consideringly at the tone of her voice, and he took out a cigarette and lit it before he answered her. "So far my company has been primarily developmental. In the past few years I have designed quite a few electronic components that have proven to be very adaptable. And we have marketed them on a small scale and done extremely well. But the chip I told you about—"

"The integrated-circuit memory chip that will hold twice as much data as anything currently on the market?"

He smiled his approval at her. And she found it meant much too much to her.

"Right. At the same size and accessible at the same speed. Well, it has the potential to be phenomenally successful, and if I were to market it myself, my company could stand to make millions."

"That's very exciting, Christopher."

"I suppose," he said, nodding as if the amount of money he mentioned were negligible. "But the excitement for me is in the development, and I've already done that. I would just as soon license someone else to manufacture it for me, and use the royalties to get on with my next project."

"But all that money!"

"You won't believe this, Lisa, but I've already made my first million." At her stunned expression, he gave a short laugh and went on. "I knew I could once I got rolling. That's why I used to work so hard." He stopped speaking for a moment and took a long draw on his cigarette.

It lay there between them. The fact that four years ago they hadn't been able to communicate their needs or their hopes and dreams to each other. If only she had been able to listen to him then as she was listening to him now, she thought despairingly. How different things would be. They could have had the shared experience of four exhilarating, growing years. But neither one of them had been able to see past his own pride.

"Anyway," he continued, "here's where you'd come in. I'd need you to act as an agent for me, to negotiate a sale price, plus royalties on every chip manufactured."

Despite herself, Lisa felt a shiver of excitement at the opportunity she was now being presented to work closely with Christopher. But she felt compelled to point out, "You could do that yourself."

"I could," he agreed, exhaling another cloud of veiling smoke. "And I'm a businessman to a certain extent. I have to be. But mainly I'm an engineer. That's where my heart is. And my next

project has already captured my imagination. I
have neither the time nor the patience to deal
with the inquiries and offers or the intricacies
involved in negotiating."

Lisa looked down at her hand; her fingers pleated
and repleated her napkin. She asked very softly,
"Why me, Christopher?"

"Several reasons," he stated coolly. "One is the
fact that you were raised practically at William's
knee. I think you've absorbed more than the aver-
age lawyer will ever know about computers, just
through osmosis."

"Perhaps," she said with a frown, willing to
concede the point to him. "You said there were
several reasons. What's another?"

"I want us to spend more time together, and it
was in my power to make it easy for us."

"I'm not sure I'm following you." She realized
she was mangling the napkin, and dropped it.
"You mean the time we will spend working together?"

All at once, Christopher appeared to become
absorbed in the depths of his brandy. "As it stands
now, we're approximately forty-five minutes apart,
depending on the time of day and the traffic.
Naturally, if you decide to accept my offer, you'll
be staying up there."

"Up there?"

"You can stay at my place. I've got quite a lot of
room, you know."

"No, I didn't, actually," Lisa murmured weakly,

trying to think very fast and having no luck at all. "I'm not sure that would be such a good idea and I really wouldn't mind the drive. It wouldn't be bad at all. A lot of people have to commute longer than that every day."

Christopher harshly dismissed the whole idea with a brusque wave of his hand. "It would be a senseless waste of time, when it's not necessary, and you know it."

"I suppose." Lisa reached for the napkin again. "What about . . ." She licked her lips. "What about Catherine?"

"Catherine?"

"You remember." Her voice took on a hard edge that she was only faintly aware of. "The 'lovely widow.' "

His green eyes studied her broodingly. "When I got back from Baja, I broke off that relationship, Lisa."

It felt as if her heartbeat had skidded precariously, then revved into high gear. "Why?"

"You used to know me, Lisa. Quite well. Do you honestly think I could make love with you like I did that night on the cliff and then come home and marry another woman?"

"No. No, I guess not." She noticed the trembling in her voice and took a sustaining drink of her coffee. Too bad she hadn't had the foresight to order a brandy too.

"What about you? Have you made your decision concerning Robert?"

Raising her eyes to his, she found that she couldn't maintain the disturbing contact. She lowered her gaze, and her words could barely be heard. "The same thing. I told him that . . . that I couldn't marry him."

Christopher reclined farther back in his chair, giving her a long and thoughtful look.

Lisa hurried on. "But getting back to the subject of where I would stay, I still have no intention of staying in your home. You must have some motels up there."

"We have one. It's out on the highway, not too far from my company, actually."

"Well, then, if I come, that's where I'll stay."

"*If* you come?"

"It all sounds very interesting, Christopher," she said slowly. "It really does. And I suppose I'm flattered that you thought of me to help you. But I'm not at all convinced I should accept."

"Why not?"

"Christopher, we met again by accident. In Baja it was very easy to get caught up in the past. But yesterday is gone."

"I don't want it back."

That gave her a momentary, painful pause. "Christopher, listen to me. Have you thought about what would have happened if we hadn't met again?"

He returned her gaze steadily but didn't say anything. She tried again. "It was mere chance. If you and I hadn't decided to take a vacation at the same time and at the same place, our decisions might have been a whole lot different."

His large hand closed over hers and the ravaged napkin. "But we did meet. And we did make love. And it was beautiful. More beautiful than it had ever been before. And you can't deny it."

No, she couldn't. Not when she was melting inside just remembering that star-bright night. "You're right. I can't. But Baja was a time out of place. No phones, no pressures. It was wonderful, but I think we'd better leave it alone and not expect anything else."

"You're afraid."

She remained silent. He was right on the money with that guess.

"It will only be for about five or six weeks, Lisa. Don't you think maybe we owe this time to ourselves?"

Lisa gave some thought to what Christopher had said. Putting it into perspective, six weeks wasn't a terribly long time. What did he think was going to happen in that length of time?

It was hard for her to believe that he was interested in a strictly business relationship. Yet she supposed it was possible.

Could it be that he was only interested in an affair for six weeks? If he was, he was going to an awful lot of trouble. Somehow that rationale just didn't make sense.

In a far corner of her mind, something at once hopeful and self-destructive whispered, "Maybe he wants to marry you again." *No!* Lisa refused to allow herself even to consider the possibility. They had failed miserably at their marriage the first time. She wouldn't allow herself to believe he could be considering it a second time for them. She knew *she* certainly wasn't.

"Okay, Christopher, I'll do the work for you. But I'll be staying at the motel."

"Good. When can you come?"

"Well, I have some things to clear up at the office, and I need to go see Uncle William. I guess I can be up there in two or three days."

"Good," he said again.

Seven

The next evening found her in front of the massive iron gates that guarded her uncle William's estate. Rolling down her car window, she pushed a button under a speaker. "May I help you?" The words were spoken in a flawless simulation of a perfect upper-crust English accent.

"This is Lisa, Ozgood. Open the gate please."

"Certainly," the voice intoned.

The gates swung open, and Lisa drove up the rounded drive to the tall front door of the old, three-story structure. Her uncle was a semiretired, fully eccentric genius in the field of electronics. Lately he seemed to be spending less and less time at his company and more and more time in his workshop, on the third floor of his house. Lisa often teased him about being a mad scientist working fiendishly in his garret laboratory, constructing evil-looking instruments that would one day take over the world . . . *if* most of the top floor of a mansion could be called a garret.

Walking up the steps, she pressed a button identical to the one at the gate. The same voice asked, "May I help you?"

Lisa, long used to her uncle's security system, replied, "Ozgood, this is Lisa. Open the door please." The system had a copy of her voice print, but she always had to speak again at the door as an added security measure.

The door swung inward, and Lisa entered an empty hallway. Proceeding down it, she peered into various rooms along the way. "Ozgood, are you here?"

A muted mechanical drone greeted her ears, and then Ozgood, Uncle William's butler, rolled into view, carrying a tray that held a glass of iced tea. "Good evening, Lisa. William told me when to expect you, and I prepared this drink for you."

Ozgood was a five-and-a-half-foot combination of metal and advanced electronics. As human-appearing as one could make a robot, he wore a black tie and tails, Uncle William's idea of proper attire for a butler.

"Oh, thank you, Ozgood." Lisa took the drink from him. She never felt foolish talking to what was in reality a mini-computer. It was as Christopher had said: Having spent a lot of time with her uncle while growing up, she had been talking to strange-looking objects and receiving varying degrees of response for years. Like Pavlov's dog, she had been conditioned, she supposed.

Handing Ozgood a container of take-out fried chicken, she asked, "Keep this warm for us, will you? It's our dinner."

Ozgood deftly slid open a panel on his stomach and popped in the bucket. After the panel was closed to his satisfaction, he asked, "When do you wish it to be served, Lisa?"

"We'll let you know later. Where's Uncle William?"

"Follow me and I will take you to him."

He led her into an open elevator. A seductively feminine voice inquired, "Floor, please?"

"Three." Ozgood all but snapped out the command. The blatant invitation in "her" voice seemed to have grated on Ozgood's reserved programming, judging from the way he responded. Lisa chuckled.

The elevator swished softly upward, and the door parted to reveal a lab that would be the envy of any research scientist—even taking into account that it always looked as if a bomb had been recently exploded in it.

Three main frames and scores of disk drives and controllers were placed around the room. Across one wall a long metal workbench presided, and over it were scattered various wire-wrap tools, sockets, proto-type boards, chips, diagrams, and schematics. Three monitors and four user terminals were set randomly about, both at work stations and on the floor. One of them was currently displaying the last move in a chess game that had been going on for months between Uncle William and the computer.

Four printers were ranged across another wall, two of them currently spewing out substantial additions to the towering stacks of computer print-out scattered randomly around the special flooring. Gingerly Lisa made her way through the untidy jumble of paper, once again comparing its ever-increasing volume to the growth of some horror-film monster.

Two mechanical munchkins, whom she had christened Frank and Stein some years ago, greeted her with a flurry of beeps and flashing lights. Approximately two feet high, they were identical, with the exception of the blue light on top of Frank and the red light on top of Stein.

"Hi, guys. Where's the mad scientist?"

"He's repairing Main frame Number Three," they responded simultaneously.

"Oh." She searched the area but couldn't see her uncle. "What's wrong with the demonic brain?"

"Main frame Number Three has a serious malfunction in the mathematical-function area," they responded. Their monotone response and lack of personality were indicative of the fact that these were variations of one of Uncle William's earlier models. Robotics wasn't his primary field, but he played around with it just to amuse himself.

"Uncle William?" she called.

He probably couldn't hear her over the clatter of

the printers, she decided, and tried again. "*Uncle William!*"

He rose from behind one of the main frames, where he had been sitting on the floor, and his vague expression sharpened to delight. "Lisa, you're back!" Walking hurriedly toward her, he held out his arms. She went into them and returned his hug, reflecting on the fact that she had always received unconditional love from this wonderful man, even when he didn't approve of what she did . . . like when she had decided to divorce Christopher.

She pulled away and smiled knowingly. "Been up to anything devious while I was gone?"

He shook his head. "Oh, no. Nothing at all extraordinary."

Lisa laughed, knowing that her uncle's idea of extraordinary was not most people's. As a matter of fact, he didn't think anything he did was extraordinary. "Have I ever told you how glad I am that you're on our side?" She faked a look of horror. "Uncle William! You *are* on our side, aren't you?"

He joined in her laughter. "Just a minute." He turned to the waiting butler. "Ozgood, turn off printers One and Two for me, please." As the robot trundled off to do this task, William turned back to her. "Now we won't have to shout over that racket. Let's go sit down"—he pointed to a sitting area more or less cleared of electronic equipment and accompanying paraphernalia—"and you can tell me all about your vacation. Did you have a nice time?"

Lisa cleared her throat nervously, uncertain about quite where to start. "Yes," she responded automatically. "Lots of sunshine and rest."

"Good food, too, I hope. There are a lot of nice places to eat down there if you know where to look."

"Yes." Lisa nodded dutifully. "Good food."

"Tell me, did Christopher take you to that restaurant I recommended, about ten minutes south of the cabin?"

"Yes, we went there one—*wait a minute!*" Her blue eyes narrowed on her uncle. "You *knew* we were both going to be down there at the same time?"

A sheepish expression crossed his face, and he reached up to adjust his glasses—a sure sign he was stalling or nervous or both. "Uh, well, actually—"

"And you didn't warn me? Oh, Uncle William, how could you?"

"Uh, I guess I thought . . ."

The light suddenly dawned on Lisa. "Uncle William! *You told Christopher I was going to be down at the cabin, didn't you?*"

"Well, let's see, now. I might have mentioned it. I really can't seem to recall. You know how busy I am. Uh . . . didn't Christopher say anything about it to you?"

"No, but you're going to. Come on," she said,

her voice full of exasperation. "You might as well confess. I can always instruct Ozgood to query your visitor log. Christopher must have paid you a visit sometime after I accepted your invitation to stay at the cabin. Sometime in the last month or two, right? And you just couldn't resist the chance to meddle."

"Well, now, I wouldn't exactly put it that way, my dear." He took a handkerchief out of his back pocket and proceeded to clean his already-clean glasses.

"No?" she questioned wryly. "Just how would you put it, then?"

"Christopher did come over one evening. You're right about that, I guess. And, let's see . . . uh. . . ."

"Uncle William," she said warningly.

"And in the course of the conversation—you know, Lisa, I always talk about you to everyone. I'm very proud of you—"

"Uncle William."

"Yes, well, as I was saying, perhaps he asked about you and maybe I did just *happen* to mention that you were going down to the cabin."

"He said you had nothing to do with his renting that house."

"Oh, he's absolutely right about that." Uncle William nodded in affirmation and replaced his glasses. "He knows the Monroes even better than I do, and has been their guest on several occasions."

Lisa gazed off into space. What did this mean?

Christopher had known she was going to be down there and he had come anyway. *He had known!*

"I thought you kids deserved another chance," her uncle was saying.

"We're not kids anymore, Uncle William," Lisa pointed out, forcibly bringing herself back to the present. "We've both grown up a lot. It's just too bad that it's so late."

Eight

Peering out of the motel window, Lisa saw that her "view" encompassed the Golden State Freeway, with its conflux of whizzing cars and trucks. She had checked in about half an hour before and had already completed her unpacking.

Even though she had called Christopher that morning to tell him that she had wound things up at the law firm and would be driving out that evening, she also had made a definite point of telling him she would see him the next morning. Lisa felt she needed this evening to think about the unsettling events that had transpired since her first day in Baja—an exercise she had avidly avoided since her return.

Worriedly she ran a hand through her auburn curls. She *really* wasn't sure she had done the right thing in accepting Christopher's job offer. Actually, she wasn't sure about *anything* anymore. What had happened to the cool lady lawyer who had her life together, Lisa had no idea. She glanced over her shoulder at the television, sorely tempted to turn it on and try to forget about the turmoil her mind was in.

Swiveling back to the room, which was furnished in the worst nondescript "Early Motel" she had ever seen, Lisa threw herself face down on the bed and cried out, "What in the world am I doing here?"

For the first time since that black-magic night on the cliff, she allowed her mind free rein. Thoughts and emotions moved and collided, and the answer came to her almost too quickly. *You're in love with the man, you fool.*

Lisa gave an agonized groan and rolled over, throwing one arm across her eyes. She was in love with Christopher, and she couldn't deny it any longer. The reason she hadn't wanted to give the matter too much thought was clear now. It was because she had known that she loved him all along.

She hadn't had a chance, not from the first moment she had seen him on the cliff. Oh, Lord, what was she going to do now? She couldn't work day in and day out for six solid weeks with a man she loved and who had once been her husband, and stay sane. But how could she get out of it? And to be honest, she had to ask herself, did she really want to get out of it? If she stayed, she would at least have six more weeks of his company.

Perhaps sanity was a small price to pay. Perhaps she had already paid it.

A knock on the door made her raise up on her elbows and eye the door with a frown.

"Lisa, it's me, Christopher." His voice came to her, muffled, through the thickness of the door.

Christopher? At this particular moment, he was the very person she didn't want to see. Scooting off the bed with her frown still in place, she edged toward the door; and as she did, she nervously smoothed the sides of the white gabardine slacks she had changed into after work, then checked the knot of the pale pink shirt tied at her waist.

Taking a deep breath, she jerked open the door. Christopher rocked back on his heels, his arms crossed over a lightweight sweater of jade green, his long, lean legs encased in well-fitting jeans.

"Oh, hello." She tried to keep her voice even and without emotion. "What are you doing here? I didn't expect to see you tonight."

"Good evening, Lisa." He strode into the room, immediately filling it with the crackling electricity that was uniquely his. "Are you settled in yet?"

Shutting the door, she leaned back against it in an attempt to allow her heartbeat to slow down to normal. "I suppose so. Why?"

"Because I've come to take you to dinner."

"Absolutely not!" She came away from the door and crossed swiftly to the other side of the room, to the mirrored vanity. *There really wasn't very much space in this room.* "I told you that I was going to take tonight to unpack and that I would see you in the morning."

His dark green eyes followed her. "So what's the problem? You're already unpacked."

"Look, Christopher, I—"

Before she realized what he was doing, she was in his arms and his mouth was on hers in a kiss filled with power. His tongue thoroughly searched out the sweetness of her mouth, thrusting deeply, probing every crevice and robbing her of strength. It seemed to go on and on, with her tongue rasping against his with an abrasive heat. Eventually he pulled back. His chest rose and fell with reaction to the passion that had flamed between them the moment their lips had touched, but his half-closed eyes gave nothing away.

"Why did you do that?" she asked breathily.

"Your mouth was open," he pointed out huskily, "and I just couldn't resist."

"I was *trying* to talk to you, Christopher."

"What you were doing was turning down my dinner invitation, and I couldn't allow that."

Breaking out of his grasp, Lisa charged, "You're impossible, Christopher Saxon! Whatever you're up to, it's not going to work. I *know* you. Just remember, I was married to you for two years."

"Oh, I remember. I just wasn't sure you did, that's all."

She gave a frustrated sigh. *Couldn't she ever win with this man?* "What is it that you want?"

"To take you to dinner."

She looked at him uncertainly. "That's all?"

"That's all." He nodded solemnly.

"Are you sure?"

He smiled at her, yet she couldn't help but observe that his eyes were lit with a suspicious glitter. "I'm sure."

"Why did you decide to locate your company in Valencia?" Lisa asked curiously. The evening was still young, and the sky retained much of the light from the day. But she hardly noticed. There was Christopher's chiseled profile to look at; there were his strong and well-shaped hands firmly grasping the steering wheel to observe.

"Several reasons," he said, "desirable location being foremost, I suppose. This valley separates the San Fernando Valley and the Los Angeles Basin from the Mojave Desert and the San Joaquin Valley. It's convenient to everything, yet infinitely less congested than L.A. Plus there was space for my company to expand physically, and I found the perfect spot to build my house."

His house. During the first idyllic months of their marriage, they had spent countless hours dreaming of the perfect home they would someday build together. How it hurt that he had done it without her. Clenching her hands together in her lap, she said quietly, "I'd like to see it sometime."

He cast an enigmatic glance toward her, then returned his eyes to the road. "You will. Tonight, as a matter of fact."

"Tonight! What are you talking about? I thought we were going to dinner."

"We are, at my home. I'm going to grill you the best steak you ever ate."

"Now, wait a minute, Christopher. I'm not sure this is such a good idea." As much as she wanted to see his home, she knew it would be much safer for them to be with other people. Lisa was fast learning that the charged emotions that materialized every time they looked at each other were highly volatile and could explode without warning.

"It's an excellent idea. And anyway, it's too late to argue because we're nearly there."

For the first time Lisa noticed her surroundings. They had been winding their way up a canyon for the last few minutes, and she hadn't even been aware of it.

Atop the canyon sat a rambling house with multilevel decks and patios and a red-tiled roof. It looked out toward a small, private valley, with a mountain view in the background.

"It's beautiful," Lisa breathed, then turned back to him. "You designed this yourself?"

"Don't act so surprised." He laughed. "I *am* capable of doing other things besides working with integrated circuits."

"I never doubted it. It's just that in the past you didn't show much interest in anything else."

"Maybe I didn't feel the need," he countered softly. "After all, I had you back then."

Christopher got out of the car and walked around

to her side to help her out. He led her up a set of steps to two tall, heavily-carved front doors. Inserting his key into the brass lock, he thrust one of the doors open.

When she walked in, Lisa's gaze was immediately drawn to the opposite wall, of glass, some sixty feet away. Thoroughly enchanted, she started toward it.

The setting sun was throwing glints of gold into a swimming pool of sparkling blue and was casting orange fire onto the hill across the valley.

Christopher's muscled arm came around her and slid open the glass door. Outside, Lisa walked to the edge of the patio. A solid blanket of ice plant spilled away from her in an eye-pleasing but practical solution to the erosion problem. The flowers, deep purple in color, matched the distant mountains. It was a top-of-the-world vista, and she could see for miles.

Her blue eyes gleaming with awe, Lisa turned. "Christopher, I'm overwhelmed. You must love living up here. It's so beautiful and so peaceful."

"That it is," he agreed with a pleased expression on his face. "And I never get tired of the view. It's constantly changing. There always seems to be something new to see."

Back inside, the relaxed, contemporary elegance of the house seemed to welcome her. The rhythm and textures of the valley were repeated in the colors and fabrics used in the house.

"Can I get you something to drink before dinner?" Christopher inquired as he walked to the customized bar. "I'm going to have a glass of wine."

"That sounds good. I'll have the same, if you don't mind."

He poured the wine into chilled glasses and handed one to her, somehow managing to brush his fingers against hers as he did. Before she could recover from the shock of the heat that sliced through her at his touch, he raised his wineglass to hers. "To the future. May it bring us both what we most desire."

"To the future," Lisa repeated.

The tremulous quality of her voice made Christopher hesitate momentarily in the act of taking a drink, but soon half the wine in his glass was gone and he was setting it down. "I guess I'd better get that steak I promised you on the grill."

"Can I do anything to help?"

"You can set the table, the one over by the window," he directed, pointing to a round glass table, with comfortable-looking chairs that were covered in tan suede. "And make some of that special salad dressing of yours. I've missed it."

Lisa rubbed a hand over her stomach and laughed ruefully. "You *do* cook a good steak, Christopher. I can't remember when I've eaten so much."

"Thank you very much." He inclined his head

in acknowledgment of her compliment. "It's always nice to be appreciated. And let me return the praise. Your salad dressing was even better than I remembered it."

Evening had fallen, and with it a gentle breeze had sprung up, making the air cooler. The pool lights, evidently hooked up to a timer, had come on, as had the lamps that outlined the patio and provided colored pinpoints of light in the hushed darkness of the night.

Christopher had started a fire in the great stone fireplace before they had sat down to dinner. Along with the candles flickering in the center of the table, the combination den and eating area had taken on an suggestive atmosphere of intimate sensuality.

Or perhaps, Lisa mused wryly, it was only the reaction of her highly sensitive nerves to the situation. Christopher didn't seem to be in the least bit affected. Or did he?

He stood up and walked a little ways away from the table. His back was to her as he gazed across to the fireplace and drew on a cigarette. "How do you feel about tomorrow?" he asked.

"Tomorrow?" Her brow pleated in bewilderment. "What do you mean?"

"Coming to work for me."

Lisa blinked, finding it difficult to hone in on his train of thought. She was suddenly ruefully aware that the job had somehow taken a back seat to the relationship between her and Christopher. But she tried to be as honest as she could. "I'm excited"—she paused to take a drink of her wine, giving herself a little more time to think about her answer—"but at the same time I can't help but be a little apprehensive."

He turned and looked at her thoughtfully. "I think that's natural for anyone embarking on something new."

"I suppose you're right. I *am* looking forward to it, though, and it will certainly be a challenge, since I haven't done anything like it before." She paused. "There is one thing that really bothers me."

"I can't imagine what it could be."

His remark was thrown out with such lofty confidence that Lisa glared at him. Everything had always seemed to come so easily to him, and here she was, falling right in with his plans again. Her tone was sharp enough to cut as she said, "It's the fact that I'm the boss's ex-wife. I just hope there's no tension because of it."

He slowly covered the distance to her, stopping briefly by an end table to stub out his cigarette in an ashtray. "Why should something like that worry you?"

"I guess because I feel a little strange about it," she admitted, her defensiveness starting to crumble now that he was so close. "You have to admit that there are a lot of divorced men and women who can't even speak civilly to their exes."

He took her hand and pulled her up. "We'll make it just fine, Lisa," he murmured deeply.

"How can you be so sure?" She tried to search his eyes for some sign of what he was feeling. What she found was a dark light burning in the green depths.

"Because I think we understand each other better than we ever have before and because I think we're slowly developing a new respect for each other."

His voice was husky with suppressed emotion, and an unbidden shudder of emotion danced up her spine.

"Maybe," she whispered.

Lisa knew she wasn't moving and that there was space between their bodies, yet her flesh seemed to be silently reaching out for his.

"We're going to be okay, Lisa." Christopher leaned toward her, and she could smell the mingled scents of smoke and wine and his cologne. "And do you know why?"

She silently shook her head, her blue eyes fixed hypnotically on his.

"Because we both want it too badly."

The velvet texture of his voice stroked her, and her whole body was trembling for him. "What?"

There was silence for the space of a heartbeat; then he pulled her to him roughly and muttered, "This, for starters."

Lisa's first thought was to resist, but the thought

never had a chance to become reality. It was no use. His body knew hers too well, and when his mouth touched hers in a shatteringly delicate caress, so in contrast to the way his hands were moving over her body, her will became his.

His fingers dug into the pliant muscles of her bottom, bringing her hard against his pelvis, and she felt herself dissolving against him.

"God, Lisa, I should take you to my bedroom, but I don't think I can wait that long."

He swung her up into his arms and carried her to a sofa of deep plush. Lisa sank into its velvet depths and waited for Christopher to join her.

His hands were trembling as he unbuttoned his shirt, Lisa noted with satisfaction. He wanted her as much as she wanted him. She knew she should probably be unbuttoning her own clothes, but she couldn't seem to tear her eyes away from him. He flung off his shirt, exposing the golden-brown expanse of his chest. Then his fingers went to the waistband of his jeans, and with a snap and a pull, they were off in a matter of seconds.

Lisa gasped at the physical impact his nakedness had on her nervous system. Erotic warmth flowed into her loins, and her breath was coming in short, shallow pants.

Her arms reached up and circled him as he came down beside her. There was a glowing certainty within her that she loved him, and it made her all the more responsive.

His mouth went to the exposed skin at the top of the V of her blouse, and at the same time his fingers undid the knot at her waist.

Lisa's hips writhed as his hand found one of her breasts under her shirt. Gently kneading the softness of the swelling, uptilted globe with his fingers, his lips kissed their way up her throat to her mouth, where they fastened onto hers and his tongue dipped into the moist cavern he found waiting for him.

Excitement raced through her at an alarming speed, and she gave a soft little moan and arched her hips once more. She wanted him, *oh, how she wanted him.*

Then his mouth was on her blouse, softly biting her pointed nipple through the material, while at the same time his hand massaged the flesh underneath the blouse with a roughly gentle pressure. The two entirely different sensations were sparking hot bolts of electricity within her.

"Christopher, oh, please, Christopher!"

In a second her blouse was tugged open, the buttons flying off in various directions at the force of his action. He used a little more restraint when it came to getting her slacks off, but not much, and soon she was lying naked and quivering under him.

He pushed himself high up inside the waiting moist depths of her body, and she cried out hoarsely at the joy of the action. With both of them so ready, it didn't take long before they both lost control. And Christopher's hard-driving thrusts rapidly carried them into a world where there were only wondrous sensations and each other.

Nine

Lisa found that when one is lying in the arms of one's ex-husband for only the second time in four years, one tends to have trouble falling asleep. Even after he has made love to you with dazzling completeness. Or maybe, she thought, that should be, most *especially* after he has made love to you with dazzling completeness.

Lisa stirred restlessly within the confines of Christopher's arms. He was sound asleep. Without looking at him she knew because she could hear the peaceful steadiness of his breathing. If she closed her eyes and pretended, she could even imagine that it was six years ago and a time when the two of them had been blissfully happy, a time before they had let the world crowd in on them with too many pressures.

Yet, given the chance to go back six years, Lisa decided she wouldn't. That would mean she would have to relive the last four years, too, and she never, ever wanted to go through something that painful again.

So that left her with the present. On the whole, the present was rather a nice place, really, Lisa reflected, listening once again to Christopher's even breathing. The only thing was—what was going to happen tomorrow? And thinking about it long enough, the uncertainty of "tomorrow" could scare the living daylights out of her.

All things considered, Lisa mused, the best a person could do would be to try to forget about yesterday's mistakes, ignore the terrors of tomorrow, and take each day as it came.

That was what she was going to do. For the next five or six weeks, she would take whatever Christopher offered. And at the end of that time, if it was needed, she would have a graceful way out. After all, she had her job and her apartment . . . and Patricio.

Patricio! Should she tell Christopher about the boy and her plans to adopt him? Probably. But then again, why? Why do it before she saw what was going to happen between the two of them? It might turn out that her adoption of Patricio wouldn't have anything at all to do with Christopher. Not if they went their separate ways in six weeks. No, she decided, it would be better to wait.

"Lisa, aren't you comfortable?" Christopher's low voice feathered the auburn hair that lay over her ear.

She turned her head so that she could see him. "I'm fine. Why do you ask?"

"I thought you'd be asleep by now. We're sort of cramped on this couch."

She gave a soft laugh. "After four years of sleeping alone, do you think I'm going to complain about having to sleep close to you?"

He pulled her tighter against him, not saying anything. But the silence coming from him was vibrant.

Lisa knew exactly what was going on in his mind. He was wondering if she had slept alone *every* night of the last four years. She also knew that he wouldn't ask her, because the truth of the matter was that he didn't really want to know.

Lisa understood this well, because the same thing was going on in her mind. She dismissed the past. After all, hadn't she just decided to forget about yesterday's mistakes and pain?

She felt him gently brush some hair off her forehead. "The fire has died down. Why don't we go to bed?"

"Bed?" She stretched, wanting to prolong the inevitable, then she lay her head on his chest.

"There are only a few hours until dawn now" —his words were rumbled in a low growl against her ear—"and if we don't get some sleep, you and I aren't going to be worth anything tomorrow."

"You're right," Lisa agreed regretfully. "I suppose I had better get back to the motel."

"Who said anything about you going back to the motel?"

"You just said—"

"I said, why don't we go to bed?—*my* bed."

"But my clothes. All I have here is a pair of slacks and a blouse with no buttons on it. Unless you have a very relaxed dress code in your company, I think I had better come up with some more clothes before I put in an appearance."

She felt his chest move with his quiet laughter. "The slacks would be fine, but I'm afraid I would have to draw the line at the blouse with no buttons. I don't want anyone else but me seeing those beautiful breasts of yours."

His hand came out to cover the area he was speaking of, and his thumb lightly flicked back and forth across the hard point of her nipple. A pleasurable tingle skimmed over her skin at his possessive action and words.

"I gather you have a solution to our problem, then?" She tried to keep her tone light, but she found herself speaking in a whisper. Her throat had suddenly become choked with a renewed surge of desire.

"I do," he murmured huskily, taking the rigid tip and rolling it between his thumb and finger. "I'll drive you to the motel first thing in the morning so that you can change your clothes, and then I'll take you to work."

Lisa's answer was a soft moan, interspersed with

words of agreement. "Ahhhh . . . That sounds—that feels so good!—fine."

And when his teeth replaced his thumb and finger, Lisa forgot all about the subject of work and clothes.

They never made it to Christopher's bedroom; but, surprisingly, they both awoke early and with no traces of fatigue. After taking a quick shower, Lisa dressed in her clothes from the night before; and even though she managed to tie the blouse so that she was fairly well covered, Christopher insisted that she wear one of his sweaters over it until they reached the motel.

They arrived at Saxon Electronics only an hour and a half late, laughingly congratulating each other on how fast they had gotten to work. Neither one of them mentioned how they had had to take another shower at the motel because, somehow, Lisa's getting undressed and dressed again had turned into a joint venture. But the knowledge was there in their eyes as they looked at each other.

Saxon Electronics owned ten acres of prime land in the middle of Valencia's industrial district. Several buildings were already sprawled over a small portion of the land, and Lisa could see signs of expansion in progress.

Christopher guided Lisa on a whirlwind tour, introducing her to a large group of people, whose names she would never be able to remember from just one mention.

But the two she did remember were Steve, the cheerful, enthusiastic young man to whom she had spoken on the phone, and Mary, Christopher's secretary, who looked at her with curious but nonetheless friendly brown eyes.

He showed her his personal work area, where state-of-the-art equipment was very much in evidence. It was all quite impressive and she found that the excitement of the people who worked for Christopher, along with their utter devotion to him and his visionary ideas, was contagious.

"Can you tell me a little bit about what you're doing now?" she asked.

"I'd be more than happy to," he assured her, his green eyes glittering with his pleasure at her interest. "I'm going to be heading in a slightly different direction than I ever have before. You see, I've gotten interested in the development of bionic memory."

"What in the world is bionic memory?" she questioned with astonishment. "It sounds very futuristic."

"Don't feel alone. The vast majority of people have no idea what it is. It's a virgin field, literally wide open. That's why it's so exciting."

She crossed her arms over her chest, and her eyes twinkled at his almost boyish excitement. "In other words, it challenges your imagination."

He regarded her with an unsettling tenderness.

"I'm sure four years of separation has increased our understanding of each other."

Lisa could feel color rising her face. "It . . . it rather seems that way, doesn't it?"

"Yes," he murmured, his eyes lingering intimately on her face. "Well, at any rate, back to bionic memory. Briefly, it has to do with DNA chains, memory storage, and how better to stimulate the human brain through computer technology."

He chuckled at the expression of total mystification on her face. "Come on"—he held out his hand to her—"there'll be plenty of time for you to learn whatever you want to know about the subject. Right now, let me show you to your office."

The tour ended in the bright, spacious room that would be hers for the next few weeks. He watched her as she walked around the office, inspecting the appointments.

"Is everything all right? Can you think of anything else you might need?"

"No." She smiled at him and sank into the leather chair behind the wide walnut desk, which was already covered with papers. "Everything looks great. But if you don't mind, I'd like to take this opportunity to talk with you about what I'm going to be doing in the next few weeks."

"Certainly, Lisa," he agreed softly as he sat down on the corner of the desk and leaned toward her. "I have all the time in the world for you."

He certainly knew how to fluster her, Lisa reflected with amused exasperation. "Okay." She

forced a more businesslike quality into her voice.
"Tell me exactly how you would like me to handle
this for you."

He nodded. "I've already sent out feelers to various companies. As far as I know, they're some of
the best in the business. I described my chip in
detail and outlined what I want. The letter was
brief and to the point, because I honestly didn't
feel I needed to give my chip a hard sell. And I was
right"—he waved a hand toward the papers on
her desk—"because quite a few of the companies
have already responded with proposals.

"You will have complete authority to weed through
these, decide which you think are the best offers,
and then enter into negotiations for me."

"At some point, you'll want to see them, won't
you? Have me go through the ones I've chosen
and have me explain the reasons why I think we
should turn the others down?"

"Nope. I told you, I don't want to be bothered
with the details."

"Christopher, it wouldn't exactly be the details I
would be going over with you. I really feel that you
should understand what decisions I'm making
along the way and why I'm making them. The
ultimate decision will be yours, of course."

"Nope," he said again. "You will make the final
decision."

Lisa sank back in the chair, amazed. "That's
quite a responsibility you're putting on my shoul-

ders, Christopher. Would you mind telling me why?"

He tapped a cigarette out of a pack, pausing to light it before he answered. "I suppose there are quite a few reasons I could give you. One of the reasons is, as I told you, I've lost interest in the chip now that it's fully developed. But the main reason is that I have complete confidence in your ability to negotiate the best possible contract for me."

"Now." He stood up. "If that's all, I have some things to do. After work, I'll take you back to the motel, help you pack and load up your car, and then you can follow me in your car to my house."

"Your house?" Lisa fervently wished that she didn't always feel so slow around Christopher.

"My house," he repeated firmly, on his way to the door. "You're moving in with me this evening."

Lisa's days, spent close to Christopher, passed in a haze of happiness, and her nights, spent in his arms, sped by in a fog of intense pleasure. Before she knew it, half the time had gone by and only three weeks remained of her stay with Christopher.

Staring out the kitchen window to the pool, where Christopher and Uncle William were playing a game of water volley ball, Lisa was paying scant attention to the salad she was tossing. Instead she was concentrating her energies on holding back the tears that threatened to erupt. She couldn't bear to think that this wonderful period in her life was rapidly coming to an end. She tried to shrug away the thought. It was one of those dreaded "tomorrows" raising its ugly head. Resolutely she pushed it away and turned to smile at her father, who was just coming through the back door.

"Why aren't you in the pool, Father? It looks like Christopher could use some help."

He threw a wry glance at her. "You know as well as I do that Christopher is deliberately holding back in order to make William feel good. Besides, I'm too old for that sort of nonsense."

"Oh, come on. Maybe some people might buy that, but I happen to know that only two years separate you and Uncle William," she reminded him with a mocking grin.

He chuckled self-deprecatingly. "I'm afraid that I've always been too old, even when I was younger. At any rate, I'm enjoying myself. It was awfully nice of you to invite William and me to dinner this afternoon, Lisa. I must admit that my Sundays can seem pretty long at times."

"It was Christopher's idea, Father. Actually, I was a little surprised when he suggested it."

Her father arched his eyebrows in wonder. "I guess I owe him an apology, Lisa. I realize now I was too hard on him."

She laid the big wooden fork and spoon across the salad bowl and reached for a dishcloth to wipe her hands. "Don't worry about it. He's done very well since our divorce," she said, a trace of sadness tinging her voice. "Who knows if he would have done as well if I had stayed married to him?"

"Of course he would!" her father asserted sternly. "And I can see that now." There was a brief silence, and then he added, "Lisa, I was a little shocked when I learned that you have been living with him these last few weeks. I didn't really know what to think. But I can see for myself now that you're very happy, and I've come to understand that that is the most important thing—not someone else's expectations of your life."

Lisa reached for the counter to support herself. "As happy as I am, Father, it's only temporary."

"What makes you say that?"

"None of this was planned." She waved one hand vaguely. "It just sort of happened, but neither Christopher nor I ever mention the future."

"And do you think it's going to be worth it in the long run?" he asked shrewdly.

"I can't look at it like that. I'm due back at the law firm in two or three weeks, and until then I'm trying to take one day at a time."

Her father gazed thoughtfully out the window for a minute. "Have you told him about your plans to adopt the little boy?"

"No." She pushed herself away from the counter and walked around it to stand beside him. "I've thought about it, but I finally decided that there's really no reason to."

"Maybe he's waiting for you to," he suggested.

"Why don't you mention Patricio to him and see how he reacts?"

"Maybe. I don't know. Up to now I've felt it best to keep the two issues of Christopher and Patricio separate. There's such a delicate balance between the two of us, I just have a feeling that for the moment I shouldn't do anything to tip the scales one way or the other."

"One of you is going to have to lower that damnable pride you both have so much of, and address the future."

Lisa put her arm through his and asked in a teasing voice, "Pride? Shall we talk about pride, Father?"

He refused to be drawn in. "You can say whatever you want to, Lisa, but the fact remains that I've learned a lot in the past few years, watching you try to make a new life for yourself. No matter how you tried to fool yourself, I could see that you weren't happy. And I'm telling you right now that you'll never be happy until you get rid of that pride of yours and understand that the answer to your happiness is Christopher."

The afternoon passed pleasantly, with the two older men leaving soon after dinner. After they had gone, Lisa spent a little while in the kitchen cleaning up and giving a good deal of thought to what her father had said. Maybe he was right. Maybe she should tell Christopher about her plans to adopt Patricio.

But, fear of upsetting the status quo aside, there

was also another fear. If Christopher *was* thinking of the two of them getting back together, the idea of a child might completely turn him off. When she had first told Robert about Patricio, he had been horrified at the idea of having a child to raise. True, in the end he had modified his stance somewhat, but she had a feeling that that was only because he was confident that he could eventually talk her out of it. He couldn't have, of course. Her devotion to Patricio couldn't be altered.

She glanced up from the sink she was scouring to find that Christopher, who was out on the patio cleaning the grill, was nearly through. She finished hurriedly, wiped her hands off, and went out to join him.

"Hi," he called. "The kitchen done?"

"It's as done as it's going to get tonight. How about the grill?"

"The same." He grinned. "What do you say we relax for a while and enjoy what's left of the dusk?"

"Good idea." She dropped into a lounger and waited until he had settled onto the one beside her. "I think the afternoon was a great success."

"So do I," he agreed. "It was good to see your father again."

She looked at him. "You really mean that, don't you?"

He nodded. "It surprised me, too, but your father seems to have changed since the last time I saw him. I can't quite put my finger on it. Maybe 'mellowed' would be the right word."

"Like all of us, he's getting older, and perhaps sensing his own mortality."

"Right. I've been meaning to talk to you about how old you are!" Christopher reached for her hand and laced his fingers through hers.

"One thing about it," she returned saucily, wrinkling her nose at him, "no matter how old I get, you'll always be older."

"Thanks a lot for reminding me." He kissed the back of her hand and returned it to her lap. "I guess what I'm trying to say is that when a person gets older, he reflects on the past, and I think that's what your father has done. I think he realizes now that he made some mistakes with you."

Lisa closed her eyes, wrestling with the decision of whether or not to bring up Patricio. She spoke absently. "To be fair, it was hard on him, raising me alone, as he had to after my mother died."

"I suppose a person can't help but make mistakes when he raises children."

Lisa's eyes flew open. She couldn't believe it. He had just given her the perfect opening. "R-remember how we used to talk about having a houseful of kids?"

"Yes," he said slowly. "But we decided to wait. I guess that's one thing we did right. It wouldn't have been fair for us to have brought a child into the world, and then have only a broken home to offer."

Lisa swallowed hard and murmured, "Maybe in some cases half a home is better than none."

He didn't seem to hear her, appearing to be lost in his own train of thought. "A child is a big decision that involves an enormous responsibility. If two people are considering it, they should think long and hard, and not just jump into it."

Even though a knot of dread had settled into her chest, Lisa persevered. "I can't think of anything nicer than having a child."

"Under the right circumstances, I agree with you."

"What do you mean?" she asked, not sure she wanted to hear the answer.

"I mean"—Lisa noticed that his voice had taken on a vaguely troubled inflection—"that a couple should be very sure that they've got their own lives together before they think about taking on the responsibility for another life."

"I suppose," she whispered, while her heart sank hopelessly. Christopher obviously had some very definite ideas on the subject of children.

Picking up her hand once again, he smiled softly at her. "You and I have come a long way, Lisa, but we need to be careful and take one step at a time. We don't want to repeat the same mistakes."

Lisa swallowed hard. By rights, she should be feeling a tremendous surge of elation. This was the first time he had given any indication that he was thinking in terms of a future with her.

Nonetheless, she experienced no such elation. Instead, she felt as if she were being pulled apart—a paper doll being slowly rent in two. Damn it! She shouldn't be put into a position where she would have to choose between Christopher and Patricio; yet this was exactly the direction in which all the signs were pointing.

Her heart rebelled and cried out, *"Not yet."* After all, she still had some time left; and as long as that was true, wasn't there still hope?

The first part of the foundation had been laid, but it was still very weak. She would do nothing to risk its collapse. Not yet. She would wait and see.

Ten

One afternoon, a few days later, Steve popped his head around her office door. "Care for a cup of coffee?"

"I'd love one," Lisa said enthusiastically, as the aroma of coffee from the two cups he held in his hands had already reached her. "Come on in. I get so caught up in this work, I tend to forget the time. I don't think I've even had a break today."

"Don't work so hard," he cautioned, his mouth twisting into a lopsided grin. "Slow down or you'll be through before you know it, and then you'll have to leave." Steve had an open, happy face that said life had treated him kindly thus far, and Lisa enjoyed him immensely. He handed her one of the cups and sat down.

"I'm afraid it's almost over anyway. I can only stretch it out so far."

"Don't be so hasty. The Santa Clarita Valley is

growing by leaps and bounds. The opportunities for a good lawyer like you are open-ended."

Lisa shook her head and laughingly changed the subject. "I've been wanting to thank you for that bit of investigative research you did for me on Lanceco."

"No problem," the young man assured her cheerfully. "I enjoyed it."

"I don't know how you could enjoy looking through musty stacks of back issues of professional magazines."

"I'm just kinky that way, I guess. I love to read. Was the information helpful?"

"Invaluable." She paused to take a sip of the hot coffee. "That, along with a few selected phone calls, proved what I had—" Lisa stopped in midsentence at the sight of the man who had just appeared behind Steve. "Robert!" She put her coffee down and stood up to walk around the desk. "What are you doing here?"

Taking her outstretched hands in his, he kissed her on the cheek. "I had a couple of hours off today, so I thought I'd drive up and see how you were doing. I also brought you some messages and mail."

"That's wonderful. What a lovely surprise. Come in and sit down."

Belatedly remembering Steve, Lisa introduced the two men. "Nice to meet you," Steve acknowledged with a speculative look at Robert. Almost immediately, he began backing out the door. "If you'll excuse me, my break time is about up. See you later, Lisa."

" 'Bye, Steve. And thanks again." Instead of going back to her desk, Lisa indicated a chair for Robert to sit in and then took the one beside it. "Now, what's all this about having a couple of hours off? I know you well enough to realize that, unless they're purposely scheduled, you rarely have a couple of idle hours."

Robert's brow furrowed. "I've been worried about you, Lisa. The few times we've talked on the phone, you've sidestepped any discussion except on those subjects that concern the law firm." He shrugged one elegantly-clad shoulder. "So I decided to come see for myself if you were okay."

Lisa's throat threatened to clog with tears. All of a sudden, she realized how very tired she was. In the midst of what seemed to be a complicated mess, Robert offered the security of comfort and understanding. "That's very nice of you, Robert. You don't know how much I appreciate having a friend like you."

He reached for her hand and squeezed it gently. "You know I want to be more than a friend, Lisa."

"Oh, Robert, I'm so sorry, but it's just no use. I told you that I can't marry you."

"But you seemed so confused when I last saw you. I was hoping that once you spent some time with Christopher, you'd realize—"

"You're right, I was *very* confused." She smiled sadly at him and, pulling her hand away, got up to walk to the window. "But one thing that has come out of my stay up here is that I'm no longer confused. I now know definitely that I'm still very much in love with Christopher."

"I see."

Lisa stared out the window while Robert absorbed what she had told him, and she reflected that just because she was no longer confused about whether she loved Christopher or not didn't make the situation any easier. She still felt as if she were groping her way through a dark maze.

Feeling a hand on her shoulder, she turned to face Robert. There was a question in his eyes and in his voice.

"I tried to get you at the motel, but they said you had checked out."

Her gaze didn't falter from his. "I'm staying with Christopher."

He stared at her, perplexed. "So what's the problem, Lisa? Obviously there still is one, or you wouldn't look so distraught."

"It's just that there's so much uncertainty in our relationship. I honestly don't know what's going to happen. And then there's Patricio."

"Patricio? That little boy you wanted to adopt?"

"I still do, Robert, and I'm going to. But I made that decision before I knew that Christopher and I might have a chance to get back together. I have no intention of going back on my commitment to Patricio, but I don't know quite how my decision will affect my future with Christopher."

"Haven't you told him about the boy yet?"

"I keep thinking that if I wait until I'm sure of his feelings for me, everything will automatically be simplified."

Robert put his hand under her chin and raised her eyes to his. "Do you believe that?"

"I'm not sure," she admitted with a sigh.

"Lisa, I just got off the phone with David Lance, and—"

Robert took his hand away from her face, and they both turned toward Christopher, who had just walked into the office. Lisa had no idea what his expression had been before he had seen the two of them together, but at the moment it looked like thunder.

"Excuse me." His voice cut the air between them with sarcasm. "I had no idea you were entertaining. I was under the impression that this was a *business* office."

"Don't be ridiculous," Lisa snapped, the already-tenuous hold on her emotions threatening to give way.

"It's all right," Robert said. "I was just leaving." He turned back to Lisa for a moment. "If you need me, you know where I am." And then, with a short nod to Christopher, he left.

Lisa grasped the back of her desk chair, trying desperately to hold on to what was left of her composure. "Is there something you wanted, Christopher?"

"Yeah. I want to know who the hell that was and why he was holding you like that."

"That was Robert Searcy, and he wasn't holding me any way."

"Robert Searcy!" His green eyes became mere slits. "It doesn't look like you did too good a job convincing him that you couldn't marry him."

"Just what do you mean by that?"

"I know when a man is about to kiss a woman, Lisa."

Her voice became ominously calm. "Do you? That's very interesting, but since we're not going to agree on this subject, maybe we should move on to the next. I believe you mentioned something about David Lance?"

"And that's another thing," Christopher stormed. "David said that you turned down their proposal."

"That's right."

"He told me the terms he had offered, and they sounded damn good."

"So?"

"He said"—his voice faltered slightly at her cold tone, but then became strong again—"he said that you didn't even give him the chance to negotiate."

"Is David Lance a friend of yours?"

"Not exactly. I've met him a few times here and there, at different business functions."

"I see. As I recall, you gave me *carte blanche* the first day I came to work for you. Of course, I realize now that I should have taken into account the fact that we had just made love several times and, as a result, were both in the first flush of what I suppose could best be described as sexual thrall. Perhaps I should have expected that once you grew tired of me, you'd feel that you would have the right to question my decision. And certainly you do. You are, after all, Saxon Electronics."

"Are you trying to tell me David lied to me? That the terms weren't as good as he said?"

"Actually, Christopher, I'm not trying to tell you a damned thing. But just for your own information, I will say that the terms the man discussed with you were probably accurate. And you're right. They were very good. Now"—she smiled sweetly at him, while at the same time reaching to pick up her purse off the desk—"you can take the rest of these proposals"—she made a wide, sweeping gesture that encompassed all the papers on her desk—"and *shove* them!"

She was out the door and striding down the hall to the front door of the building before he realized what had happened. She looked back only once, to see him still standing in the doorway of her office, his hands on his hips, watching her.

Lisa kicked out into a slow, leisurely breast-stroke across the pool. The movement of her body through the cool water eased the tension out of her muscles and the anger out of her bones. It was so quiet. Only the sound of a dog barking in the distance broke the silence of the afternoon.

Back and forth she stroked, until she was

exhausted. Then, flipping over on her back, she floated, with her eyes shut to the cloudless sky above her.

She drifted without thought, without worry, until she had rested. And then she turned back over to swim to the edge of the pool. Lisa climbed out and strolled to the diving board, automatically checking the straps of her blue Lycra bikini as she went, to make sure they were secure.

The springboard extended over the deep end of the pool, and after taking a practice jump, Lisa dove cleanly into the pool, making straight for the bottom. Instead of surfacing, she glided along the floor of the pool, enjoying the feeling of being in another world, where there was no sound and where there was only peace.

But at last, with her lungs nearly bursting, she regretfully surfaced to air . . . to reality . . . to Christopher. He was standing on the deck above the pool. Their eyes met and held for a moment; then he turned and walked into the house.

Aware that her limbs were shaking from the exertion of her swim, Lisa made her way through the shallow water to the submerged concrete steps of the pool. Collapsing onto the middle step, she leaned back to rest, supporting herself with her elbows against the top step.

There was a slight disturbance in the water, and she knew Christopher had settled on the step beside her.

"Lisa, I'm sorry."

His rough, soft voice brought her head around. A weight of depression lifted from her at the sight of him so close and evidently willing to talk things out. "I'm sorry too. The last thing in the world I want to do is fight with you."

His hand briefly caressed her cheek. "You've got nothing to apologize for. It was my damned temper."

"Still, I should have stayed and tried to explain. Do you want me to tell you now why I turned down Lanceco's offer?"

"No. Hell, I don't even care. I never did. I was only using David's call as an excuse to see you for a few minutes this afternoon. But when I walked in and saw Searcy tilting your chin up to him, suddenly all I could see was blazing red."

Lisa couldn't still the happiness she felt at his unconcealed jealousy. "There was no need for you to get upset, you know. Robert was only paying a friendly visit, delivering messages and mail."

The water lapped onto her bare skin, just below the line of her bikini top, as Christopher changed his position, rolling onto his side to face her.

"The farther away that man stays from you, the better I'll like it. He obviously hasn't accepted your decision."

"I *work* with Robert's firm," Lisa protested, amused. "We're bound to be together at times. And, yes, he has accepted my decision. Believe me."

"I do."

Lisa felt her breath catch at the heated look Christopher was giving her. "I still want to tell you why I turned down Lanceco. I'm sure everything that David Lance told you was the truth. Their proposal was very professionally done, and their terms were extremely generous, but there was some ambiguous wording in it that bothered me. It seemed to give them the option, if they chose to exercise it, to hold back on the production of your chip for an indefinite period of time. So I had Steve go through stacks of your professional magazines, knowing that you never read them, and I followed up his findings with telephone calls of my own. Sure enough. It seems David Lance has done just that in the past."

"But why would he want to hold back my chip, when producing it could make him so much money?"

She reached up and tugged a strand of his golden-brown hair. "I can see why you wanted someone to act as an agent for you. You're very naive in the ways of business, aren't you?"

"Never mind," he growled with mock fierceness, "just get on with the explanation."

She grinned. "Yes, sir. At any rate, if Lanceco could get control of your chip, they could keep it off the market as long as they wanted to. This would be particularly advantageous to them if they happened to have a chip of their own that's not as advanced as yours. Consequently they'd first need to deplete their own supply before yours hits the market. I checked, and guess what? They have just such a chip. If we had accepted their offer, they could have cleaned up with their own chip and then made a killing with yours."

He stared at her with amazement. "I'm impressed, Lisa. And very grateful."

A gurgle of laughter rose in her throat. "It's what you're paying me for. By the way, it won't be long before things are wound up. I've entered into negotiations with the Sylvan organization."

"Sylvan Enterprises has a good reputation." Christopher nodded absently, his gaze fixed on the distant mountains.

"That's what I've found out. But I've double-checked everything anyway. The résumé of the proposed project director was exceptionally strong. I think you're going to be pleased."

"Fine," he murmured, swiveling back to her. Lifting his fingers out of the water, he dripped a trail of water onto her skin, just above her bikini top. The cool droplets took a meandering route down into her cleavage. "What do you think of the area up here?" He again dipped his fingers into the water and then repeated the process, watching the clear streamlet as it disappeared tantalizingly into the low neckline of the blue top.

"I've told you before," she answered, then inhaled sharply as his mouth lowered to her chest and his tongue began to trace the route the drops of water had taken. He was stopped at the edge of the suit, but his mouth worked its way the short distance to her already-rigid nipple and fastened onto it through the wet Lycra.

A moan broke free of her softly parted lips. She couldn't repress it. Erotic feelings were rushing to all parts of her body. Her fingers threaded through his hair, all the better to press his face into her breast.

Her encouragement made him suck that much harder, and Lisa lay back on the stairs, half in and half out of the water, totally in his control.

At her yielding, Christopher broke away from her breast. With one hand he reached behind her to unfasten the two clasps that held the skimpy top, and with the other he delved deeply into the bottom of her bathing suit.

"By the way, you were quite wrong."

"About what?" she asked breathlessly. His hoarsely spoken words came to her as if through a fog.

"I haven't grown tired of you. I don't think I ever could."

The top came off, and he tossed it onto the decking. Then he was cradling her against him, and his mouth moved on hers with a sure possessiveness. She responded with everything that was in her. This man was her husband, and she knew she would never want another.

His fingers gently circled that softly sensitive spot between her legs, bringing her closer and closer to a much-desired brink of ecstasy. She couldn't stand it any longer. Unclasping her arms from around Christopher, she peeled her bikini down around her legs and then completely off, not caring that it floated away.

Now there was nothing except the water to hamper his fingers. As they rotated back and forth, the water slushed ever-so-lightly against her, increasing the shuddering sensations to a powerful degree.

Somehow Christopher's swimming trunks were off, or maybe he hadn't been wearing any. It didn't matter. Lisa had long since ceased to reason. She could only feel—feel the overwhelming need building inside her.

Rolling to the front of her, Christopher pulled her over him, and, with a push away from the steps, they were floating—Lisa on top of him, with his muscled body a raft.

His mouth never left hers as he propelled them into deeper water. It was incredible, Lisa thought hazily, the two of them gliding as one through the cool, silent water. But still it gave no satisfaction to her heated body.

All at once they had reached the side and she was standing upright, with her back against the wall of the pool. Using his footing on the bottom as leverage, Christopher parted her thighs and pushed into her. His hands curled around her buttocks and impelled her against him with an urgent force.

Wrapping her legs around his back, Lisa clung to him and let him drive her higher and higher, until finally they both reached the miraculous pinnacle they sought.

He held her tightly to him, matching her ragged breathing with his own. When at last their breathing had quieted, Christopher, still holding her, lay back on the water. They floated lazily together in a timeless dream, until Christopher whispered, "Let's go in the house. I have an intense desire to make love to you again. Only, this time, with us both dry."

Eleven

A few days later Christopher's secretary buzzed Lisa. She picked up the phone. "Yes?"

"There's a call for you on line two, Lisa."

"Thanks, Mary." She punched the button marked "two." "Hello?"

"Lisa, it's me."

"Robert! How nice to hear from you. Did you call to find out when I'm coming back? It shouldn't be too much longer." She didn't add that leaving Christopher and returning to her old life was going to be the single most difficult thing she had ever done. Remembering her vow to deal with it when the time came and not before, Lisa pushed it out of her mind.

"That's good to hear, Lisa. We'll all be glad to see you." Robert paused, and his voice took on a different note. "But that's not why I called."

"Oh? What's up?"

"A little while ago, one of the secretaries here

took a message for you, and since it sounded important, she decided she should bring it to me. She knows we're in touch."

Lisa felt a cold stab of apprehension. "What is it?"

"Señor Martinez, the lawyer you hired in Rosarito Beach, was trying to get in touch with you."

"Did he say why?"

"All he would say was that Patricio has evidently been hurt in some way and that he thought you should come down right away."

"Oh, no! He didn't say how? Or if Patricio's uncle had caused the injury?"

"No. That was all he said. I gather the connection wasn't that good."

"I can believe that. Knowing the erratic telephone service down there, it's a wonder he even got through."

"Lisa, are you going?"

"Absolutely. I'll leave right away. Listen, thanks a lot for calling. I really appreciate it."

"That's okay. I thought you'd want to know. Lisa?"

"Yes?"

"Are you going to tell Christopher where you're going?"

"I've got no choice now. I'll have to. Good-bye, Robert, and thanks again."

Lisa hung up and punched the button that buzzed through to Mary's desk.

"Yes, Lisa?"

"Could you tell Christopher I need to see him right away, please?"

"Oh, don't you remember? He had a luncheon appointment down in Van Nuys."

"Damn! I did forget." She picked up a pencil and began tapping out an agitated rhythm against the desk while she tried to decide what to do.

Since she didn't know how seriously Patricio had been injured, Lisa didn't feel she could afford to wait until Christopher returned. Besides, a lengthy explanation would be required, and she didn't have the time. The idea that his uncle might have hurt Patricio in some way scared her to death. Señor Salina was so used to mistreating the child that Lisa could easily see him losing his temper and seriously injuring Patricio. And there was no one down there who would stop him.

This, along with the thought of Patricio in pain, feeling alone and afraid, was enough to spur her to action. "Mary, when Christopher returns, tell him that I've had to leave town for a couple of days."

"Is there a number where he can reach you?"

"No. Just tell him not to worry, and I'll be back as soon as I can."

"Okay, but he's not going to be happy," Mary warned.

Lisa gave a short laugh. "That's probably an understatement, but it can't be helped. I'll see you when I get back."

*   *   *

Fortunately, Lisa still had the keys to Uncle William's cabin. Consequently, after a quick stop at Christopher's house, where she threw a few things into a bag, Lisa was able to drive directly there.

Arriving in Rosarito Beach by late afternoon, she drove to Señor Martinez's office, where she only stayed long enough to discover that Patricio's arm had been broken.

"How did you find out?" Lisa asked.

"I probably wouldn't have known about it, except Señor Salina decided to use it as an excuse to get more money from you. He said he needed it to pay the doctor's bill. But as far as I can determine, Señora Saxon, the uncle had nothing directly to do with the accident. Apparently the child stumbled and fell while taking out a heavy container of garbage."

"Even if Señor Salina did break Patricio's arm, we'll probably never find out," Lisa said angrily. "Patricio has developed this sort of fatalistic acceptance of his uncle's treatment of him. Did you give him the money?"

"I didn't feel I could refuse, on the off-chance that he might really need it to pay the doctor, but I insisted on giving the money directly to the doctor."

"That was very wise of you, Señor Martinez. You did the right thing. Do you think you could find a competent woman to stay with Patricio for a few days while I go back to the States and wind up some things?"

"*Sí*. My wife's cousin, Maria, would be glad of the chance to earn a little extra money."

"Good. Have her come out to my uncle William's cabin as soon as she can."

Lisa took a few minutes to open the cabin in order to air it out, and then she walked over to the cantina. She knew Patricio and his uncle lived in a room at the back of the building, and it was there that she found the boy.

"Lisa!"

He looked paler than when she had last seen him, and, if possible, maybe even a little thinner. Lisa took him in her arms. "I heard that you had broken your arm, so I came down to see if you were all right."

"I was afraid you had forgotten me," he confessed sadly.

Holding his frail body a little more tightly, Lisa exclaimed, "How could you even think that? I could never forget you! I made a promise to you, and I always keep my promises."

"My *tío* told me you would forget."

"Well, now you know otherwise." She released him so that she could see his face. "Tell me. How are you feeling? Does your arm hurt very much?"

"Not so bad. *Un poco*." He bent his head to look at his cast. "I mustn't complain."

"Now, I wonder who could have told you that?"

Lisa muttered, adding, "And more than once, I'll bet." As Patricio switched his brown eyes to her, she added, "Listen, having a broken arm entitles *anyone* to complain."

"But I can't do some of my work," he explained.

"*Some!*" she exclaimed. "I wouldn't imagine you could do much of anything for a while."

"So! *Señora*, you have returned."

Lisa swiveled to see Patricio's uncle in the doorway. "I told you I would. I also warned you about taking good care of Patricio."

"Oh, *sí*. I have. I have. His arm"—he made a disparaging gesture toward the cast—"*es nada.* It's nothing."

"You call a broken arm nothing?" Lisa gave Patricio's hand a reassuring squeeze and stood up. "Señor Salina, I'm taking Patricio back with me to the cabin."

"You cannot do that, *señora*," he protested vigorously. A strange look of panic contorted his face.

Lisa wondered briefly at it, before she agreed pleasantly, "Maybe I can't legally, but one of the wonderful things about Baja is how *loudly* money talks down here. And, if you insist on making an issue of it, I'm willing to bet that I can convince the authorities just how much better off Patricio will be away from you."

Señor Salina's expression changed to a sly, speculative one. "The adoption papers have not yet been signed, *señora*. And I haven't decided whether or not I want to sign them."

"But you will," she observed cynically. "I don't think you'll be able to turn down the amount of money I'm going to give you."

"Maybe." He shrugged indolently. "Maybe not. It depends."

"On what?" she questioned suspiciously.

"On how *great* an amount you're willing to pay. You see, *señora*, there is someone else interested in adopting Patricio."

"Who?" She threw a quick glance at Patricio, but relaxed when she saw that he seemed as surprised as she was.

"Someone whom I'm sure would be willing to give me more money."

"Nice try, Señor Salina, but I don't believe you. If you think that by telling me there's someone else, you can push up the price, you are very much mistaken. I'm already offering you twice as much as I should." She looked back at Patricio. She hated for him to have to hear this discussion, but she seemed to have no choice. "Where do you keep your things, love?"

With his good arm he pointed to a chest. "The drawer at the bottom."

Lisa reached in and easily gathered up the few articles of clothing. "Come on, Patricio, let's go." She spared one last look at Señor Salina. "After I get Patricio settled in with a woman I am hiring, I have to go back to the States for a few days. But as soon as my business is taken care of, I'll be back, and then I'm staying until the adoption is official and I can take Patricio home with me."

"You cannot do this," he blustered. "I will not allow it. I will—"

She turned a cold stare on the man. "Do whatever you feel you need to do, Señor Salina, but you will never again get your hands on Patricio." Señor Salina was still ranting as Lisa helped Patricio out the door.

During the next few days Lisa spent most of her time making sure that Patricio and Maria would have everything they needed while she was gone. She took Patricio to the doctor for a checkup, mainly to reassure herself that everything had been done that could be done for him; and as each day went by, she had the satisfaction of seeing the pinched look on Patricio's face gradually begin to disappear. He was eating well and thriving on the attention Lisa and Maria were showering on him.

Maria had turned out to be a pleasant young woman, and she and Patricio got along wonderfully. Lisa decided they would do very well until she could get back. So after giving Maria instructions to contact her cousin-in-law if Señor Salina attempted to bother them, Lisa kissed Patricio goodbye and headed for Valencia.

Maybe because Lisa knew she was going to have to face Christopher and his questions when she arrived, the trip was more exhausting than usual;

and by the time she reached Valencia, it was around three-thirty in the afternoon.

By then her nerves were clamoring and her body felt heavy with fatigue. She went directly to the house, despite the fact that she knew Christopher would be at the office, or more probably because of it.

Pulling her car into the driveway, she noticed that it was at a decidedly odd angle, but she switched the engine off anyway, grateful that she had completed the trip without a major mishap. She grabbed her bag and entered the house, coming to a stop just inside the door.

There, lounging on one of the couches, was Christopher. On the coffee table in front of him, a large ashtray brimmed over with discarded cigarettes. An assortment of glasses filled to various levels with different-colored liquids sat on the table. It was obvious that he had spent a lot of time in the same place over the last few days.

"Where the hell have you been?" Christopher stormed at her, getting off the couch with lightning speed and advancing toward her.

Her bag slipped from her hand, causing her to wince as it hit the tiled floor. Putting her fingertips to her temple, she pleaded, "Please don't yell at me, Christopher."

"Don't yell at you!" he shouted incredulously. "I'll either yell at you or beat you. Take your pick."

"How long do I have to decide?" Still massaging

her temples, Lisa very carefully made her way to the couch.

Following her, he demanded, "Damn it, Lisa. How do you expect me to react when you leave without a word and are gone for four days? I've been half out of my mind with worry."

Lisa lay her head back against the sofa and shut her eyes. "I left word. I distinctly remember telling Mary to tell you not to worry and that I would be back as soon as I could."

"Oh, great," he retorted sarcastically. "And you thought that that would ease my mind? Even though you had disappeared and no one knew where you were?"

"Christopher," Lisa whispered. "You're shouting again."

"*Lisa!*" Hazarding a glance at him, she encountered the full force of his wrath-filled eyes. Yet as they looked at each other, she could see that it was slowly getting through to him that she was terribly tired and tense. "Lisa," he repeated in a somewhat lower tone. "*Where* have you been?"

This was the moment she had been dreading, and now that it had arrived, she honestly didn't think she could cope with it. Not now.

"Christopher, I haven't had an easy trip. It's been emotionally and physically exhausting, and tomorrow I have to start drawing up the final draft of the contract between you and Sylvan Enterprises."

"*Damn the contract!*"

Deciding not to point out that he was shouting again, Lisa ignored his outburst and continued. "It won't take long, since I've already done most of the preliminary work. For now, let's just leave the subject of where I've been, and I promise you that as soon as the contract is signed, we'll sit down and talk."

His gaze had turned brooding. "Do I have a choice?"

Her lips twisted into a semblance of a smile. "Not much, with me feeling the way I do right now."

"Okay." He exhaled heavily. "How can I help you?"

"If you wouldn't mind getting me a couple of aspirin, I think I might be able to make it up the stairs and get myself to bed."

"Stay here," he commanded shortly but softly, and disappeared out of her line of vision. A minute later he reappeared with a glass of water and two aspirin. He stood in front of her while she took them, and then, after setting the glass to one side, he scooped her up in his arms and carried her to the bedroom.

With Christopher's help, it didn't take Lisa long to undress and climb into bed. As she settled her head gratefully on the pillow, her eyes were already shutting. "Thank you, Christopher."

She heard him moving around the room, drawing the drapes against the late-afternoon sunlight, and then there was the firm, cool touch of his lips against her forehead.

"I don't know whether it will help or hurt," he whispered, "but I'm going to tell you anyway—I love you."

What Christopher lacked in timing, he made up for in discretion. The next sound she heard was the closing of the door.

God help me, Lisa thought, I don't know what I'm going to do.

These past weeks with Christopher had been heaven recaptured. He loved her, she knew it now; and, given enough time, they just might have been able to make it work this time around.

Unfortunately, though, they hadn't had the time yet to cement their relationship. If they had, maybe Christopher would have been able to accept the idea of a child, even a child that wasn't theirs. The tragedy, though, was that now she didn't have anymore time to give.

She loved Christopher so. Yet how could she let Patricio down? She answered her own question: *It's simple, Lisa. You can't.*

Twelve

It had been three days since Lisa had returned from Baja, three days in which she and Christopher had treated each other with extreme wariness, carefully circling any subject that might lead to a discussion of anything more serious than the weather.

Lisa paused in her packing and looked around the bedroom, thinking that too soon it had all been over—the final negotiations, the signing. The deal had been concluded to everyone's satisfaction. The signing of the contract had taken place in her office earlier in the day, and Lisa had left soon afterward, telling Christopher she would see him at home.

Christopher had not touched her since she had returned from Baja, and in a way, Lisa was grateful. She rationalized to herself that she might as well start learning to do without his lovemaking right away, and that it might even make her departure

that much easier if she didn't have to leave with
the taste of Christopher on her lips. Yet another,
larger part of her, that part that encompassed her
whole heart, knew there was nothing that was
going to make it easy, and she yearned for his
caresses with everything that was in her.

She heard the front door slam and braced herself.
This was it. She couldn't avoid it any longer. The
time when she could put off facing the certain
reality of tomorrow was past.

She looked down to place a blouse in the suitcase, and when she looked up, he was there.

"What are you doing?"

"I'm packing."

"I can see that for myself, Lisa," he rasped
sarcastically. "What I want to know is why."

"My job is over here. It's time to go home."

"Stop packing," he ordered irritably, "and let's
sit down. We need to talk, Lisa."

Throwing a final pair of shoes in the suitcase,
she shut the lid and snapped the lock. "There. I'm
through anyway."

"Good. Let's sit over here." He indicated the two
armchairs placed at conversational angles in front
of the window. He waited until she was settled,
then he pounced. "Now, suppose you tell me just
exactly what's going on. No"—he ran a hand agi-
tatedly through his hair—"on second thought, let
me go first. Maybe it will help you understand
things better."

He paused, seeming to marshal his thoughts.

"When I left home four years ago, it was because I felt that we needed time to straighten out our lives. I thought time away from each other would give us the opportunity we needed to do this. Divorce was the last thing on my mind."

"Christopher—"

"Just a minute." He held up one hand. "Let me finish. I know now I was wrong about that—and a lot of other things too. I should have made more of an effort to talk to you, to let you know what I was feeling. But it had gotten to the point where the only time we were halfway civilized to each other was in bed, and I guess I opted for the easy way out."

He reached for his cigarettes and lit one, taking a long draw before he continued. "When the divorce papers were served on me, I got so mad that I gave you the divorce without trying to fight for you. That was another mistake, perhaps the biggest mistake of all. It wasn't until some months after the divorce had been granted that I cooled down, and by then of course it was too late.

"I rebounded, in a big way. I went from one woman to another; but it didn't seem to make any difference who I was with. I only saw you. Then I met Catherine. In her I recognized another genuinely hurting person, and I thought that by helping her, I could help myself. Needless to say, that didn't work either. I knew then that I would never be able to forget you.

"I had come to a point in my life where I had

achieved what I had set out to do professionally; and from William I knew that you were at the same point. When he told me that you were going down to the cabin to think over a marriage proposal, I jumped at the chance. I went down there to see if you might have some feelings left for me." He took a drag on his cigarette and smiled reminiscently. "After our first kiss, I knew you did.

"The rest I'm sure you've guessed. I brought you up here, not only because I knew you'd do a good job for me, but so that we could have more time together. I love you, Lisa. And I won't accept the fact that you don't love me."

"You're right," she said simply. "I love you very much. But life is rarely that uncomplicated, Christopher. And in our case things are incredibly involved."

"Involved?" He arched his brows in surprise. "Nonsense! What could be simpler than the fact that we love each other? If you're worried about your law practice—"

"I'm not. Steve has already thrown out broad hints about this valley's need for good lawyers."

"Well, then, what are you talking about? I can't imagine anything important enough to interfere with our spending the rest of our lives together. Lisa, *I want you to marry me.*"

How ironic, Lisa thought, that she should feel sadness upon hearing him say the one thing she most wanted to hear. She stood up and walked over to the bed. "I'm afraid there *is* something important enough to interfere, and it has to do with the trip I made a couple of days ago."

He frowned and ground out his cigarette. "What are you talking about?"

She took a deep, sustaining breath. "I'm talking about a seven-year-old boy named Patricio, who lives in Baja. I am going to adopt him."

Christopher couldn't have looked more stunned than if he had just been struck by lightning. *"You're kidding!"*

If she had harbored any hopes that he might be willing to accept Patricio, she had just had her answer. "No," she said sadly. "I'm not. You see, I decided to adopt him before I realized that I was still in love with you and that we might have a chance to get back together. To be truthful, though, I don't know whether it would have made any difference if I had known. I still would have wanted to adopt him. It's just that I would have talked it over with you."

She looked at him one more time. He sat very still, looking rather strange, as if he couldn't quite take it in. Picking up her suitcase, she said, "Good-bye."

"Wait . . . Lisa, please."

"No, Christopher. I've got to go back down to Baja. I'll be staying down there until the adoption is final, so I don't suppose I'll be seeing you again."

She paused, but he didn't say anything more. He just kept looking at her in that peculiar way. She turned and walked out the door.

Lisa sat on the porch of the cabin, watching Patricio throw pieces of stale bread out to the sea gulls. He was rapidly coming to terms with his cast, only complaining now and then about how his arm itched underneath it.

She smiled, hearing Patricio laugh with glee as a sea gull swooped particularly low to catch a crumb in midair. The sound was like music. He laughed more and more now, and if she had her way, he would always laugh like that.

Having been back in Baja for a little less than a week, Lisa had accepted her future. If she couldn't have the ecstasy of a life with Christopher, at least she would have the satisfaction of providing a good one for Patricio.

She rolled her shoulders to ease her tension a little and glanced toward the cantina. This afternoon Señor Salina would sign Patricio's adoption papers. Lisa was determined. He had been dragging his heels long enough, giving her lawyer a hard time, but today she wasn't going to take no for an answer, and there was no time like the present, Lisa decided. She needed to catch him before he had to start cooking for the dinner customers.

"Patricio," she called, "tell Maria I'm going for a walk, and you stay close to the cabin. Okay?"

Patricio nodded happily, engrossed in his game with the sea gulls.

She found Señor Salina sitting behind the cantina in the same place where he had been when she'd first seen him. He was even sitting in the same position, with his chair propped up against the adobe wall. An awful lot had happened since that morning, she reflected, yet here he sat as if everything was the same.

"Good morning, Señor Salina."

He raised his head and looked at her, then dropped his chin back on his chest. "*Señora,*" he mumbled.

"Señor Salina, I've brought Patricio's adoption papers for you to sign."

Without moving, he said, "I told you I wasn't sure—"

"How can you live with yourself?" Her voice was raised in frustration. "You're his uncle. Since you don't want him, it seems to me you'd be glad that I want to give him a good home."

Señor Salina raised his head again to glare at her. "I *told* you, *señora,* someone else wants Patricio."

"And I told *you, señor,* that you're not going to get one more penny out of me, so you might as well quit bluffing and sign these papers." She thrust the papers out and rattled them. "I know there's nobody else."

"Look, *señora—*"

"Do as the lady says, Salina. Sign the papers."

The terse command was given by a voice that was very familiar to Lisa. Momentary confusion roiled through her. A tiny flare of hope lit up in her, then died. It couldn't be.

She whirled to face Christopher. "What are you doing here?"

She heard the thud as Señor Salina's chair hit the ground, and then he was brushing past her. "*Señor!*" he gushed ingratiatingly. "*Señor,* you're back!" He turned to Lisa, beaming with the first smile she'd ever seen on his face. "I told you someone else wanted Patricio."

"I don't understand." Lisa looked at the two men in bewilderment.

"Sign the papers," Christopher repeated, his sharp gaze still on the other man. "Because you're not getting any more from me."

"But *señor*—"

"Christopher, what's going on here?"

His expression softened as it switched to her. "Hello."

"What are you doing here? What does he mean about someone else's wanting Patricio?"

"I've missed you."

"Christopher, answer me!"

He took the papers out of her hand and thrust them in front of Señor Salina along with a pen. "Sign!"

"But *señor, no comprende.* I thought you said *you* wanted Patricio. You gave me money and everything."

"I said I had to talk to my wife first," Christopher said.

"Your wife!" Lisa exclaimed.

He put his arm around her and drew her to him. "My soon-to-be-again-and-forevermore wife, Señora Saxon."

"Su esposa!"

"And we are going to adopt Patricio," Christopher continued. "But you will get no more money than what my wife has already offered you. Now, sign!"

Señor Salina signed the papers with an unsteady hand. As soon as he was finished, Christopher took them and gave them to Lisa. "Thank you, Señor Salina. Our lawyer will be in touch with you."

The pressure of his arm made Lisa move, and they began walking. She wasn't sure what was happening, except that she had the papers and they were signed. "Christopher, where are we going? What's happening here? I have no idea what you're doing here or what you have to do with Salina."

"We're going down on the beach so that we can be alone."

"But why?" she sputtered. "I thought—"

He stopped, and cupped her face with his hands. "Lisa, my darling, do you have any idea how beautiful you look right now or how much I've missed you?"

"Christopher—"

"Come on. I was at the cabin before I came over here. I told Maria and Patricio to expect us when they see us. We've got some things to talk about, and the sooner we get down to the beach, the sooner you'll understand everything."

Nothing was making any sense, but Lisa meekly followed him down the cliff. Once at the bottom, they paused to take off their shoes. Then he led her to the jetty, where he saw to it that she was comfortably positioned in the lee.

Six years ago, on their honeymoon, they had spent hours in this very spot. Weeks ago she had sat here, trying to forget him. Now they were here again together. Life had a way of coming full circle, Lisa thought as Christopher sat down beside her and took her hand in his.

"From the first moment I saw you on this beach weeks ago, I knew I wanted to live out the rest of my days with you. You'll never know the restraint I used. But I had made too many mistakes in the past with you, and this time I was determined it would be forever.

"During that time I, too, made friends with Patricio. I felt immediately that he was a wonderful little boy, caught in a terrible situation, and I wanted to take him out of it more than anything."

Lisa couldn't believe her ears. Unable to speak, she could only look at him in astonishment.

He smiled at her understandingly. "But first I had to win you back and then discuss it with you. So I gave Salina some money along with strict instructions to take good care of Patricio until I could get back. I didn't dare talk it over with the boy for fear of getting his hopes up and then having something happen. I wanted him, but I wanted you more."

Lisa shook her head. "I can't believe it."

"Now you know how I felt. When I came home from the office the other day, to find you packing to leave, I went into an instant panic. I knew we had a lot to talk over, but when I saw you standing by your suitcase, all of a sudden I didn't know what to say to you to make you stay.

"So I talked about what I knew—our past, and my past without you—trying to make you understand that I saw the mistakes I had made. But it seemed to make no difference, even though you said you loved me. I couldn't understand it, until you told me about Patricio. And then I was totally and absolutely shocked. Never in my wildest dreams did I think that you might have met Patricio and grown to love him as I had."

"But why didn't you say something?" Lisa asked.

"I couldn't; I was too stunned. And then you left before I could gather my wits. If you had stayed just a few more minutes, you would have heard me start to laugh. I couldn't believe the wonderful coincidence. It just showed me all the more that we were meant to be together."

"But why did you wait so long to come down here and tell me all this?"

"Because I wanted these last five days to be our

last separation. You had said you were going to stay here until the adoption was final, so I knew I had time to square things away at work. Now we can be married and honeymoon down here while we wait for the okay to take Patricio back with us."

Tears filled Lisa's eyes. "Do you have any idea how happy this makes me?" she questioned.

"I know how happy it makes me. To say that I've been a little worried these past weeks would be putting it mildly. I not only worried about whether I could make you love me again, but I worried about what you'd think about the idea of adopting Patricio."

"But that night after Father and Uncle William left, we talked about having children."

"I did most of the talking, if you'll remember. It seemed to me that you were reluctant to talk. Or maybe the subject troubled me so much that I just didn't hear what you were trying to say."

"Oh, Christopher, I love you."

"Hush, now. We can talk some more later. For right now . . ." His mouth lowered to hers, and their lips touched. The ocean rolled on, the earth turned, and the stars were appearing one by one in the heavens over the Baja coast before the kiss ended.

THE EDITOR'S CORNER

As Mrs. Denise L. Miller, Warner Robbins, Georgia, wrote to us about LOVESWEPT heroes, "they should be ruled dangerous to the readers' hearts and minds. I for one have fallen in love with quite a few of the leading men...." What a wonderful comment! And we're so pleased to bring you four more love stories next month with irresistibly lovable heroes, the kind who put us in mind of yet another quote. This one comes from that famous lady, Mae West: "It's not the men in your life that count, it's the life in your men!" So, here's a brief description of the LOVESWEPT romances you have to look forward to next month, described chiefly by their lively and lovable heroes.

First, Nancy Holder gives us one of the most charming of lovers in **THE GREATEST SHOW ON EARTH,** LOVESWEPT #47. Evan Kessel is like no bank loan officer I ever met! He's tall, tanned, has seal-black hair, blue eyes ... and a secret little boy wish to run away and join the circus. You guessed it, I'll bet—heroine Melinda Franklin owns a wonderful old-time circus. But poor Evan! He has to do his courting over the blaring of Guido Zamboni's calliope and the antics of two chimps named Marcel and Marceau. And when Melinda throws herself at him, it is only from the bar of a flying trapeze. **THE GREATEST SHOW ON EARTH** is a deliciously romantic confection!

(continued)

Speaking of chimps, when patent attorney Laurel Brett Fortier meets her new client, a toy inventor named Thane Prescott, he's wearing a gorilla suit! Now Thane is a little offbeat to be sure, but not so bizarre a man that he chooses to dress in costume . . . it's just that the zipper is stuck. And he can't get out of the suit even when he's preparing to meet Laurel's very stuffy, very conservative family—her father the judge and her brothers the lawyers. What a clash of lifestyles and what merriment ensues as true love blossoms . . . even to the squawking of handsome Thane's foul-mouthed parrot in Sara Orwig's wonderfully humorous **BEWARE THE WIZARD,** LOVESWEPT #48.

When opportunity and Jessica Winslow knocked, Ethan Jamieson seized the moment . . . and the lady in his arms. Never one to miss an opportunity in business or romance, this sensitive entrepreneur knew he'd found a neighbor to share his life forever. But there were misunderstandings galore to overcome. First, he thought Jess was a snoopy opportunist; then Jess thought he was an unscrupulous materialist. Sorting it all out makes for a touching and delightful romance. We're very, very pleased to be able to present yet another talented new author to you. Kathleen Downes makes a most memorable debut with **THE MAN NEXT DOOR,** LOVESWEPT #49.

Brent Taylor is one of Noelle Berry McCue's most delectable heroes. A foreign correspondent who has faced death in every corner of the earth where there's been a dangerous assignment to cover, Brent captivated his foster sister's heart when Joy was just seventeen. **IN SEARCH OF JOY** opens with the heroine a much more mature woman, but still mad about the dashing Brent who has come home at last. We feel sure that this poignant love story, LOVESWEPT #50, will captivate you.

As always, we send you our heartfelt thanks for the wonderful response you've given to each and every one of the LOVESWEPT authors and those of us on the staff.

With every good wish,

Sincerely,

Carolyn Nichols

Carolyn Nichols
  Editor
LOVESWEPT
Bantam Books, Inc.
666 Fifth Avenue
New York, NY 10103

LOVESWEPT

Love Stories you'll never forget by authors you'll always remember

☐	21503	**Heaven's Price #1** Sandra Brown	$1.95
☐	21604	**Surrender #2** Helen Mittermeyer	$1.95
☐	21600	**The Joining Stone #3** Noelle Berry McCue	$1.95
☐	21601	**Silver Miracles #4** Fayrene Preston	$1.95
☐	21605	**Matching Wits #5** Carla Neggers	$1.95
☐	21606	**A Love for All Time #6** Dorothy Garlock	$1.95
☐	21607	**A Tryst With Mr. Lincoln? #7** Billie Green	$1.95
☐	21602	**Temptation's Sting #8** Helen Conrad	$1.95
☐	21608	**December 32nd . . . And Always #9** Marie Michael	$1.95
☐	21609	**Hard Drivin' Man #10** Nancy Carlson	$1.95
☐	21610	**Beloved Intruder #11** Noelle Berry McCue	$1.95
☐	21611	**Hunter's Payne #12** Joan J. Domning	$1.95
☐	21618	**Tiger Lady #13** Joan Domning	$1.95
☐	21613	**Stormy Vows #14** Iris Johansen	$1.95
☐	21614	**Brief Delight #15** Helen Mittermeyer	$1.95
☐	21616	**A Very Reluctant Knight #16** Billie Green	$1.95
☐	21617	**Tempest at Sea #17** Iris Johansen	$1.95
☐	21619	**Autumn Flames #18** Sara Orwig	$1.95
☐	21620	**Pfarr Lake Affair #19** Joan Domning	$1.95
☐	21621	**Heart on a String #20** Carla Neggers	$1.95
☐	21622	**The Seduction of Jason #21** Fayrene Preston	$1.95
☐	21623	**Breakfast In Bed #22** Sandra Brown	$1.95
☐	21624	**Taking Savannah #23** Becky Combs	$1.95
☐	21625	**The Reluctant Lark #24** Iris Johansen	$1.95

Prices and availability subject to change without notice.

LOVESWEPT

Love Stories you'll never forget by authors you'll always remember

SPECIAL
MONEY SAVING
OFFER

Now you can have an up-to-date listing of Bantam's hundreds of titles plus take advantage of our unique and exciting bonus book offer. A special offer which gives you the opportunity to purchase a Bantam book for only 50¢. Here's how!

By ordering any five books at the regular price per order, you can also choose any other single book listed (up to a $4.95 value) for just 50¢. Some restrictions do apply, but for further details why not send for Bantam's listing of titles today!

Just send us your name and address plus 50¢ to defray the postage and handling costs.
